MIDNIGHT FOR A CURSE

MIDNIGHT FOR A CURSE

A Curse Keeper, Curse Breaker Fairytale

E.J. KITCHENS

Brier Road Press

Midnight for a Curse / E.J. Kitchens —1st ed.

Print ISBN: 978-0-9993509-3-5

❀ Created with Vellum

To all those who've put up with my constant chatter and questions about my books and covers and character names—this one is for you

PROLOGUE

I had to grant a wish by midnight. In hindsight, I made a poor choice of a "fairy goddaughter." But, you see, I'm an enchantress, not a fairy at all, so I shouldn't even have to grant wishes and such. Real fairies don't. Only that black-hearted mischief maker Prince Dokar of the Unseelie Realm takes pleasure in interacting with mortals. But as I was saying, I sometimes have to grant wishes, so don't blame me if things go awry on occasion.

—LADY VIOLETTA, *Enchantress*

CHAPTER 1

Once upon a time there was a beast who loved nothing better than to sit in a comfortable chair in a sunny spot in his library and read. He was a most unusual beast, not because he read and wore a velvet doublet as fine and well-tailored as any prince's, but because he was a prince, and though cursed, was content. At one time, he had been a human prince, an indolent, self-absorbed man who lived merely to eat and to read, much to the distress of his father the king and those who would one day be his subjects.

How did this indolent prince become a beast? Well, one fine midsummer the prince journeyed to one of his family's smaller castles in the west of the kingdom to escape his father's hounding. He had a fine supply of books there, and the resources of cheeses and fruits from the local villages were excellent. It began as a peaceful summer retreat, but then, on an unassuming Thursday, there came a determined rap on the front door. This distracting noise continued for some time, causing the prince himself to abandon a most interesting book, leave the comfortable library, and limp to the door. Mysteriously, none of the servants were about.

The prince barely gave a thought to the unsightly hag occupying the stoop and paid no notice to her plea for bread and shelter for the night. His mind full of his book and his missing servants, he merely opened the door and said, "Stop that racket at once!" Seeing that she stepped away from the knocker, he slammed the door shut and retired once more to his snug library, convinced that had solved the difficulty.

However, no sooner had he delved once more into the story than he was driven out again, this time by a burst of light that quickly dissipated, leaving an enchantress spewing a string of angry words. Astute man that he was, the prince rapidly deduced the woman was upset and begged her pardon for whatever he had done, or whatever his errant servants had neglected to do. The woman, beautiful and mysterious as such creatures often are, enigmatically declared that *his* apology— for it was he who had somehow irritated her—was too late. She settled a curse on him and his, turning him into a beast, his figuratively invisible servants into truly invisible servants, and his beautiful castle into an architectural monstrosity that matched its beast-like master. The prince must experience a change of heart, she said, to be free of the curse. He had until an enchanted rose died to do so.

However gloomy such a fate may have first appeared, the prince bore the curse very well. As did his servants. After all, there were no more visitors to disrupt the prince's reading or cause the servants extra work. And he couldn't possibly be expected to return to his father and his princely duties any time soon.

Two years passed quietly before the enchantress returned to see what effect her efforts at improving the young man had had. She found him once again in his library reading, the only difference being he no longer had a blanket over his lap, his fur now keeping him sufficiently warm. Her dismay and distress were extreme, but she was unwilling to admit defeat —or perhaps she feared the king would not pay her the final amount he owed her. For he was less than satisfied with the results of her work.

After pondering the situation for a fortnight, the enchantress returned and added new terms to the curse: the prince must venture forth from his castle once every morning and present himself at the boundaries of his land, where the villagers could see him. He must ask any young woman he was in company with to marry him. Their rejections, she was sure, would humble him and speed up his change of heart.

She reminded him of his timetable, of the enchanted rose now in full bloom minus a few petals, and once again admonished him to have a change of heart. As the brilliant flash of colors from her departure faded, a petal fell from the rose. With it fell the prince's hopes of a quiet, literary life.

🙙🙚

BELINDA LAMBTON DASHED into the woods. The deep, dark woods, where, if she were lucky, she'd get lost.

"Belinda, sweetie pie! Where are you?" yelled a smooth voice that could only have come from one particular handsome face.

Belinda hiked up her skirts and pumped her legs harder. When would her father come back and tell that arrogant jackanapes that when Belinda said she wouldn't marry him, it wasn't feminine coyness, it was the honest-to-goodness truth?

The woods grew denser and gloomier as Belinda wove in and out of the trees with quiet steps. At the stirring of leaves she changed directions and ducked into the cover of a large and thick cedar, where she collided with a warm, furry blanket. That promptly screamed.

Belinda screamed too and leapt out of the cedar, bumping into the creature again as it chased her out. She kicked it firmly in the shins and ran for dear life.

A bear! She'd nearly been eaten by a bear!

Belinda's heart pounded as she darted left and then right in a zigzag pattern to confound the brute behind her. Was not-marrying Gaspard really worth being eaten by a bear?

"Lindie pie? Are you all right?" Gaspard cried from somewhere to her left.

Yes. Yes, it was.

Belinda skidded to a stop and tucked herself into the hollow of an ancient tree partially hidden by a rhododendron, her own private cave she'd found a few weeks before. Scarcely daring to breathe, she pressed herself against the damp wooden shell until the sound of heavy footfalls passed her by.

Once, then twice. Gaspard coming and going, she hoped.

After some minutes of quiet, she peeked around the stiff rhododendron leaves, saw only peaceful nature, and ventured from her sanctuary. She finally dared a deep breath, reveling in the feel of lungs full of fresh air.

Judging from the sun, it was about time for Gaspard to return to the butcher shop. She stretched her arms, letting out a great sigh. "Congratulations, Belinda. You've survived another morning. Now only ..." Was it six weeks remaining before she could expect her father's return, *if* things were on schedule?

Groaning, she started for the village. She snagged an oak leaf off a low bough and tore it to shreds as she walked. It was a pity she hadn't brought her bow. She could've caught fresh meat for herself, preventing the need to venture any further into the market than the herb dealer she would sell her plunder to. With a smug smile, she patted the satchel resting against her hip. These trips into the forest to avoid Gaspard had produced some reward.

Crunch.

Belinda froze in the shadow of a pine.

Crunch.

Gaspard hadn't given up on her.

Restraining an unladylike word, she backed slowly around the tree, her gaze searching for her tormentor. And then she bumped into something firm, but not rough and hard like a branch. Soft fur tickled her neck, and a blood-curdling scream found its way out of her mouth.

The funny thing was—and she must be going hysterical even to think it—was that the meeting had a similar effect on her attacker, for it shrieked likewise. Even as she lunged forward with another cry of her own, she quailed at the noise *it* made in return. It could be nothing less than the yell of a creature raising its courage to slay her, but it sounded almost like a cry of terror equal to her own.

Gathering her pluck, she snatched a fallen branch and spun. But the sight of the creature was too much for her. Her arms stilled, branch raised.

A giant, hairy beast stared at her through wide blue eyes, eyes the color of a mountain lake on a sunny day. They looked almost human. It blinked, drawing her attention back to the fur surrounding its eyes. It was trying to mesmerize her with its gaze and then eat her.

Arms quaking, she filled her lungs with more air for a scream to break the spell of its eyes.

It raised its gigantic paws to its cat-like ears, great tufts of auburn hair sticking straight up above them. "Please not again," it said in a low, rumbly voice.

Belinda stiffened. Had fright damaged her senses, making her hear words in a dumb roar? She opened her mouth again.

It scrunched its face. "Please."

Please? She slowly lowered the branch. "What did you say?"

Its blue eyes widened. "I mean, '*Roar*.'" Curving its massive paws in front of it, it lurched toward her, sharp claws glimmering in the sunlight.

Mouth agape, Belinda stepped back, her foot twisting on a fallen limb. Dropping her branch, she landed on the ground with an *oomph*.

"Oh my," the creature said. It stepped forward as if to help her up, then seemed to think better of it and returned to its aggressive position and roared.

There was something familiar about that pose. Belinda blinked, a sly smile forming on her face. It was a monster's storybook illustration pose.

She tucked her smile away for later. An old wise woman once told her to follow the story at her feet. This was a very large story and would be easy enough to follow. "Well, don't just stand there, Mr. Monster, help me up," she said sharply. It took all her restraint to keep from smiling at the startled look on the creature's face.

It put its hands on its hips. "I shall not. You should be running for your life."

She extended her hand. "I am, for life and freedom. Now help me up."

It arched a great patch of light fur, possibly the equivalent of an eyebrow. Then, it growled and grabbed her arm and helped her up. "All right. But it's only to give you a head start. I like to keep my hunting sporting."

"Oh, Beastie! Where are you?" A high-pitched, saccharine-coated, feminine voice made Belinda cringe worse than the hairy paws that had pulled her gently up.

The creature shivered, sending loose fur wafting down to the ground and onto Belinda's sturdy boots. It glanced between her and the forest through which the voice had traveled. Did it just send a look pleading for her to be quiet?

"Bella pie? Sweetie. Is that you? I have lunch all laid out at the shop. It's getting cold," Gaspard called.

"Beastie, I'm over here, dear," continued the woman.

Belinda and the monster both gulped. Slowly, they backed between the branches of the pine.

When naught but a squirrel had moved for a full five minutes, Belinda let out a great breath, hissing it through her teeth. The monster followed suit.

"She gets closer every day," it said with a sigh, then murmured something Belinda couldn't make out. Clearing its throat, the monster started forward, then jerked back. With an "Oh bother. Don't let me keep you," it started peeling off its fur, making Belinda cringe, and think of the necessary preparations for the rabbits she should set a trap for. Yet the beast's peeled fur looked remarkably like a coat, its coloration and texture a perfect match to its head and hands.

The coat remained on the pine branch as the creature stepped forward. It brushed a few pine needles from its shirt-sleeves, which were pushed up to its elbows, then rolled its shoulders—under a fine velvet doublet—before carefully unsticking its coat from the branch and putting it back on. It fixed her with a fierce gaze. "Now, I'll give you a ten-second head start, just to be sporting, and then you're fair game. It *is* nearing lunchtime, after all."

Belinda eyed the monster, with his hidden suit of fine cloth, and noted the scent of lavender mixing with the tang of the pine sap dripping from the branches around them.

"All right," she said. After peeking around the edge of the branches' covering, she stepped out into the forest and swiftly crossed to the next thick tree trunk and then to the next. Then, she sneaked back to the first. Pressing herself to the trunk, she watched the creature make a cautious exit and hurry past her. Before he could disappear among the foliage, she eased from her hiding place and followed him.

He soon slowed his pace and began to swing his giant arms in rhythm, as if he were finally walking with his accustomed gait. He removed his fur coat and tossed it over his arm. Around rocky outcroppings and over dry, leaf-strewn streambeds he strode. A clump of silver-leafed hoary mint, topped with wispy pink petals, reached out from a lightly sloping bank. He snagged a silver leaf, and rubbing it, raised it to his snout just as his feet discovered the hole of a rotted-out tree stump. With a strangled yell, he tumbled to the forest floor, his fine jacket catching amid briars.

Belinda rushed forward and knelt beside him. "Do let me help you up. Just to return the favor, you know."

He jolted to a sitting position but stopped short as the briars clinging to his jacket pulled taut against their tree. "What are you doing here?" he growled as he strained against his bindings.

"Following you." Belinda grabbed a handful of jacket, making him hold still.

"Why?" he sputtered.

She didn't answer but began releasing him thorn by thorn. After a minute, during which he puffed angrily and fidgeted, she removed the last briar. With a clipped thanks, he jumped to his feet and brushed the dirt from his clothes.

He started off again, and Belinda walked by his side, studying him. He kept his gaze fixed ahead.

"You're the monster said to have eaten the prince, aren't you?" she asked at length.

He jerked to a halt and spun around to face her. "*Eaten* the prince? Really! I must say I—" He paused, mouth agape. He closed it slowly. "Yes, you're quite right. I did eat the prince. I love eating princes. Very nutritious. Full of minerals."

"Like gold and silver?"

He quirked an eyebrow. "Quite right. Eating young

women is my next favorite, however; so you should scram." He shooed her and walked on.

"Now look, Mr. Monster, I'm in a jam—"

"My name is not Mr. Monster. I really prefer Mr. Beast, or just Beast."

"So sorry. As I was saying, Beast, I'm in a pickle. This village lout called Gaspard keeps after me to marry him. He won't take no for an answer, and my father is away and so can't back me up."

"That's most unfortunate. I wish your father a speedy return. Good day." He raised his paw as if to tip a hat, then picked up his pace.

"Wait. You have a giant castle where no one goes. Why can't I stay there until my father returns?"

"Out of the question."

Belinda ran around in front of him and poked him in the chest. "Why don't I give you a ten-second head start just to be sporting, *Beastie*?"

He jerked to a halt, eyes wide. "That's not fair."

"I'm no fool. You're running away from someone same as I am. If you let me stay, I'll help you."

"No, no, no." Beast clenched his fists and marched around her. "You'll interrupt my daily routine, and I'll have to—no, certainly not."

Belinda jogged beside him. "I'll help the servants, brush up the hair you shed"—Beast glared over his shoulder at her —"keep unwanted visitors away. Anything you ask."

"Why don't you start by keeping yourself away?"

"You've got to help me. Please." Desperation edged into Belinda's voice, ruining the bossy tone, but it, or something, put a stutter in Beast's pace.

He turned to face her. "Is it that bad?"

She nodded, biting her lip.

With a growl that vibrated the ground under Belinda's feet, Beast motioned her forward. "All right. But only until your father gets back, then you must leave and promise not to tell a soul what you've seen." He muttered as he walked on, "I can't believe I'm agreeing to this."

CHAPTER 2

Belinda tried not to think as she marched alongside Beast. If she did, she might please Beast by running away. But she was too much a coward for that. Gaspard could be kind, and with six weeks before her father returned and almost no one else kind to her ... it was too dangerous to risk.

She quickened her pace as a wrought iron gate three times as tall as Beast rose suddenly before them. So soon? It'd only been a half-hour's brisk walk. She really hadn't expected a ... She foundered as she caught a glimpse of the building beyond the gates. Castle? It was the size of one but hardly the normal design. She could only describe it as a once grand tree that had been twisted by storm and gale, one continuing to grow but warped to the core. She shivered as she took it in. Privacy must definitely be a priority.

"Still with me, I see," Beast said glumly as he slowed before the castle's formidable doors. The handles bore a remarkable resemblance to their owner, and she was momentarily afraid he expected her, as a mere villager, to open them for him. However, he placed his giant paw on the handle and twisted slightly to meet her gaze.

"I wouldn't dream of abandoning you," she said with more pluck than she felt.

He huffed. "Perhaps you should. It's not too late."

"Your home is delightful in a stark, easily defensible kind of way."

He stared at her a moment, then let out a sigh of defeat that threatened to blow away her hat. He opened the door and motioned her inside. "After you."

"Thank you." Straightening her shoulders and locking her jaw in place, she entered, preparing to be unprepared for what lay inside. She did very well for the first three minutes, standing quietly beside Beast in the middle of the entryway as he rang a bell and waited for who knew what. The inside wasn't quite so intimidating as the outside but was just as impressive in size and twisted grandeur. The chandelier had to be thirty feet above her head and the entryway bigger than her father's current house. Only the desire to not appear the country bumpkin she felt—and a promise to herself to come back later and gawk properly alone—kept her calmly glancing in polite sweeps about the room, her hands clasped primly in front of her. She'd already breached protocol by calling the creature "Beast," but she couldn't give it, with all its furriness and rather adorable tufts to its cat-like ears, the title *Mister*. Now, she'd be elegant.

"Oh good. You're all assembled."

Belinda jumped as Beast straightened and directed his attention to the empty air between them and the broad staircase leading to the second floor. A quiet shuffling came from that direction, but nothing to have made it met Belinda's sharp gaze.

"Allow me to introduce you to—" He leaned toward her and whispered, "What's your name?"

"Belinda Lambton," she whispered, searching the far side of the entryway for the source of a subtle hush.

"Miss Belinda Lambton. She is a damsel in distress and will be staying here until her father returns. Please give her every consideration. Thank you. Fulton, please see that a room is prepared for Miss Lambton."

The shuffling, the brush of fabric and padding of leather soles against marble floor, rose around her, pitching Belinda's heart rate into a different sort of rhythm altogether.

She couldn't help it. She glanced around and up and down and back and forth in very bumpkin fashion, searching for the source of those sounds. Perhaps, she thought as Beast motioned to the empty room, perhaps she had made a mistake after all.

"Miss Lambton?"

Wide-eyed, she spun around to face Beast. "Yes?"

"I said 'Welcome to my home.'"

"Oh. Thank you." She curtsied, not knowing what else to do. Across the entryway, a door opened on its own.

Beast nodded regally, then turned away. "The servants will attend you. Good morning."

Belinda sprinted after him, slowing to match his pace as she slipped up beside him. "What servants?"

He froze, and Belinda could just see his eyes darting back and forth in thought before he turned fully to look at her. "The ones who greeted us so politely a moment ago, of course."

His look was too cunning by far for a beast. Belinda crossed her arms. She was not to be gotten rid of that easily. The cost of defeat was too great. "Oh, those. I assumed you meant the ghosts of the servants searching for their murdered prince."

Beast pursed his lips in irritation, which caused one fang to poke out beyond his upper lip.

Belinda's mouth twitched, her eyes unable to forgo the pleasure of laughing at that unruly fang. He caught the direction of her gaze and his own gaze dipped to his mouth. His lip popped out over the fang of its own accord. Belinda barely stifled a giggle.

Rolling his eyes, Beast spun away. "They're invisible so I don't have to watch them watching me. Come along. I'll show you to your room myself."

Still biting her lip, Belinda managed a thank you. The grin in her soul faded as Beast offered her his arm. It was a gentlemanly gesture she was little used to receiving from any but her father, and he didn't have monstrously hairy hand-paws with cougar-like claws. Swallowing hard, she touched her hand lightly to Beast's arm and told herself the fur was a glove.

"How did you know they were assembled if you can't see them?" she asked as he led her to the stairs. "Do you go by smell as—" *an animal might?* She cleared her throat. "Or by sound?"

Her trepidation eased immediately at his glower. Animals who ate people didn't glower. They just ate.

"They become a bit of a waver to you after you've been here awhile—not that you'll be here that long."

"Far be it from me to impose, Beastie dear," Belinda couldn't help but goad.

Beast sighed like a proper martyr, making Belinda struggle to contain her grin once more, but then she sobered. "I fully intend to keep my part of the bargain, you know," she said. "I really do appreciate you allowing me to stay."

He gave her a sideways glance but didn't reply as he led her along a grand hallway, a guest wing she assumed. "Lunch will be served in your room," he said at last, "as you'll likely want to rest and clean up from the adventures of the morning. Dinner will be at eight. You are free to roam the castle and grounds as you please—except into private chambers, of course."

Belinda's heart gave a strange and painful thump. She'd expected to be a servant. He'd made her a guest.

"Do you speak many languages?" he asked after a moment, a surprising amount of interest in his voice.

"None but ours fluently. Just a few words here and there my father taught me. He was a merchant once and has traveled much."

Beast slowed to a halt before a grand door decorated with a relief of blasted trees and snarling monsters. He knocked, and as the door swung open, he rattled off something at the rate of an Italian auctioneer. It may very well have been in Italian as well. *Vuoi sposarmi*, perhaps?

Belinda, whose attention had been sucked into the room beyond, turned back to him with an inquisitive expression. "Ye—"

"No!"

She jumped back at Beast's exclamation.

"Excuse me," he stammered. "I ... I wasn't really expecting an answer. I like rhetorical questions. Good morning. Please ring for the servants if you require anything." He released her arm and darted away.

"Okay," she stammered, staring after him, momentarily considering whether or not she was crazy to assume he wasn't.

She shook herself and walked into the room—her room—and winced. It was too grand for her. Even the stable was too grand after the way she forced herself on Beast's hospitality. His alarm after the mysterious woman called for him sprang to mind. She couldn't earn what she'd bullied him into giving, but she'd do whatever she could to make sure he didn't regret it. Anymore than he already did.

Sealing that vow with a jerk of her chin, she set about searching for wavers in the room, then remembered Beast had said *invisible*, not necessarily *mute*, servants. Could she send one with a note to town? She needed to hire a local youth to take care of her father's few poultry and goats while she was away, but she didn't want to sneak back herself to do so.

She discovered a maid in the room and learned of her afternoon plans: lunch, a bath, a fitting for dresses the maid seemed excited to assist in making, and then dinner with the master. She didn't get the chance to ask about her message.

TWO HOURS LATER, Belinda sighed contentedly as she wrapped a soft robe around herself and left the tub, its scented water still barely warm. Snuggling in the robe, she sat at the dresser and began to brush her tangled chestnut hair in front of the mirror. It was a bath such as she hadn't enjoyed since her more affluent childhood. She hadn't realized how much she'd missed it.

"Psst."

Belinda jumped and spun around, half gagging a scream by nearly eating the silver handle of her hairbrush.

A beautiful woman in a doorway-wide, frilly, muted gray dress stood two feet behind her, a wand in her hand. The enchantress—for what else could she be?—sighed irritably. "I purposefully did *not* make my usual dramatic entrance so you *wouldn't* scream. Do you think I like wearing drab dresses like this?"

"Is everything okay, miss?" The question followed a soft knock on the door.

Belinda glanced between the enchantress and the door through which the servant's voice passed. The lady in gray waved her hand as if indicating she should answer.

Belinda lowered the hairbrush. "Yes, thank you for checking," she said, rather louder than she meant to.

The enchantress nodded approvingly, then twisted and swished her wand behind her. A padded chair of matching color to her dress appeared, and she elegantly seated herself on it. "Has he asked you yet?"

"Asked what?"

"You to marry him?"

"Marry him! We've only just met, and I don't think he cares much for me." And she'd thought the matchmakers in her village were bad! Gaspard at least had known her for years before plaguing her. He claimed she needed him to look after her and that she was the most beautiful woman in the village. Those reasons, or a desire for the sense of status her once-wealthy father's connections might give, made her desirable to him.

The enchantress raised a sculpted brow. "You're not going to protest that he's a frightening beast?"

Belinda gave her a withering look. She might not be a bookish wench, but she was no fool. "He's not a convincing beast, no matter how much hair and teeth you've put on the poor man."

The enchantress's lips thinned. She tapped her fingers on her crossed arms. "I wouldn't exactly call him a *poor* man," she said at last. "But you didn't answer my question. Did he or did he not? He knows the rules."

Belinda's brows drew together. What kind of curse had poor Beast gotten into? "No, he didn't. Wait." Surely proposals wouldn't follow her here too? "He did mutter something in Italian earlier, but I didn't catch what he said, and he didn't explain."

The enchantress's lips pinched quite thin this time. "The cheater," she hissed. "What did you say?"

"'Okay,' but that was after he'd said a few other things."

"Hmm. You should be careful how you answer, dear, especially if you don't understand the question."

Belinda arched an eyebrow, then dipped both into a V. "Is part of his curse asking every woman he meets to marry him?" That would explain why he was so eager to avoid that woman in the forest, and herself.

"A minor part, yes. I rather hoped it would scare him into the change of heart that would break the curse. Unfortunately, he's a better runner and conniver than I expected."

Belinda's eyebrows continued in their workout, raising together in surprise this time. The enchantress ignored her for a moment, seemingly intent on some problem.

"I almost answered him, 'Yes?'" Belinda murmured after a moment of silent thought herself. Thank goodness Beast had interrupted her.

"Oh, don't do that, dear," the enchantress said, alarmed. "You'd hardly make a suitable wife. Well, perhaps with a different outfit ... I'm a fairy godmother on the side, you know. But I'll have to think it over." She eyed Belinda a moment, then gave her head a slight shake.

Ignoring the slur, Belinda continued, "Does he have to marry the one who answers him with a 'yes'? Because I almost answered 'Yes?', which isn't quite the same thing as 'Yes.' And certainly not as 'Yes!' Does it have to be a 'Yes.' or 'Yes!'? Or would an 'I do' or 'I will' or 'Yep' or 'Sure thing' or any affirmative word or phrase suffice?"

The enchantress opened her mouth, then shut it a couple of times before speaking. "I don't know. I'm not sure how particular the curse is. I've never used it before."

"Hmm," Belinda said. "Well, I appreciate the warning. Would agreeing to marry him turn me into a beast or free him?" What did the enchantress want of her?

"Neither. It was just a scare tactic that isn't working. He has to have a change of heart."

"About what?"

"Well, that's what I came to talk with you about, isn't it?"

"Oh."

"You look like a hard-working village lass."

Belinda smiled at the compliment, whether it was intended as such or not.

"The—Beast is shirking his responsibilities. His father wants him to come back, but all Beast wants to do is sit comfortably by the cozy fire and read, safe and untroubled by the responsibilities of his position."

Read. Belinda stifled a pang of jealousy. "So you want me to convince him of the value of hard work? Or make him too miserable to stay here?"

"Something like that."

Belinda cocked her head. "Why should I? He's been kind to let me stay here, though I admit I bullied him into it out of desperation. I don't want to get myself kicked out before my father returns. And what kind of a father has his son turned into a beast?"

"What kind of a father lets his son waste his life and abandon his people?"

"You have a point," Belinda conceded.

The enchantress smiled slyly. "So you'll assist me—the great enchantress Lady Violetta—in this curse breaking?"

Belinda started to agree, then clamped her mouth shut. Should she trust the enchantress? Risk getting kicked out over a family issue?

"You could say it's for the good of the kingdom, your own family." Lady Violetta gave her a cunning look. "Or you could do it for a reading spell." Her pink lips twisted in a smirk as Belinda's eyes narrowed. "You're not the only one who's clever," the enchantress continued smugly. "I know all about you, Miss Belinda Lambton. Third and youngest daughter of a former merchant, once wealthy and privileged but now confined to a country village after a series of shipping disasters ruined your family's fortune. You were the youngest of the children, but in some ways suffered more from the change than the others, though they whined more. You have difficulty reading and didn't do well in the village school. Your own sisters made fun of you because of it. When you realized you couldn't be a scholar like your sisters, who were in truth merely elegant, useless embroiderers who only read poetry to impress beaus, you became a tomboy, practically a hunter-gatherer and servant combined to help your father make ends meet. You had too much of an affluent background and beauty to be liked by the village girls and too much tomboy and too little gossip to be liked by the friends of your cousins in the city."

Belinda's hand fisted around the silver hairbrush. "What makes you so sure I want to read easily?"

Lady Violetta's lips slithered into a wily smile. "It doesn't matter. You'll need to read in your battle of wills with Beast. I suggest you start by hiding the language books; otherwise, I'll have to have a talk with him about dissembling during his proposals, and I'd rather not reveal myself at present. As for breaking the curse, consider how you'd want a leader to act. Think on that. He must stop being the indolent, self-absorbed, overgrown blanket he currently is, and the sooner the better." She rose, and the chair disappeared. "Now, I must go and you must finish your toilette. I do hope they give you better gowns—and footwear—than the ones you wore here."

"Wait," Belinda said, rising. "Who is Beast truly? Who am I to help him become?"

"You're such a clever miss; I thought you would have figured that out by now."

"I've only just met him," Belinda sputtered. There were dozens of nobles and leaders around to be potential fathers anxious for their heirs. There was also the prince and his first cousin, the king's heir and the spare. Belinda's comment about Beast eating the prince had only been to goad him and was based on a ridiculous rumor. Yet, the prince hadn't actually been seen in a while ...

Lady Violetta raised a sculpted eyebrow at Belinda, and Belinda's nose itched. She wrinkled it as discreetly as she could. Where was she? Oh, yes. Even an enchantress couldn't get away with cursing a prince. And the king's palaces were too far away from her village for the half-hour walk that brought them here. The prince hadn't been seen in a while, to be sure, but he was away somewhere looking for the man who tried to assassinate the king and who'd injured him a few years ago, and probably looking for a wife too. Beast had to be some nobleman's son.

"If I were you, dear," Lady Violetta interrupted Belinda's thoughts, "I'd focus on helping him overcome his indolence and self-absorption, for everyone's good, including your father's."

Her leading tone caught Belinda's interest. "You'll help my father if I help Beast break his curse?"

"It will certainly benefit him. I'm sure something could be arranged to that nature."

Belinda's brows furrowed at the muddled answer. "I need specifics."

Lady Violetta sighed. "I wouldn't be the one giving the benefits, but I imagine a forgiveness of remaining debts and possibly the gift of a ship and cargo or something equivalent to set him up in his profession again could be arranged."

Belinda's heart thumped in a hope painful in its unfamiliarity, but she kept her face impassive. "I left unexpectedly today and don't want to return home, even for a few minutes. Could you send a note for me to Ben Harrow, a local youth, about him caring for the poultry and goats while I'm gone? And leave a note at our house saying I'm away? I don't want anyone thinking I've been abducted. There is also a couple, the pastor and his wife, expecting me to dinner ..." Guilt knotted her chest. How could she have forgotten Lettie and Winthrop? Wonderful as they were, though, she didn't regret being free of Gaspard for six weeks.

"Of course. I'll take care of everything."

Trying to hide her relief, Belinda gave the enchantress's request one last consideration, then nodded. "I'll do what I can."

The enchantress gave her that "you'll never do" shake of her head. "If you'd said, 'I promise,' I could have given you such useful aids—a magic mirror, an enchanted rose, maybe even a traveling ring—but you—" She waved her hand dismissively in Belinda's direction and gave her head another shake. "But you have your reading spell and your domestic help, you'll have to make do with that. Well, that's settled. You're an official Curse Breaker now. May you be successful."

What good was an enchanted rose or magic mirror? "But you didn't say who—"

"Good afternoon, dear," Lady Violetta said hastily, taking up a silver watch hanging from her bodice. "Oh my. Look at the time. We'll talk later. Remember, Curse Breaker, the rose is dying." A storm-gray cloud engulfed her, and she disappeared in a flash as of lightning.

Gaping, Belinda watched as a neat square of parchment tied in gray ribbon fluttered to the floor.

Belinda picked up the parchment and opened the envelope. It contained a letter with a few lines written in an elegant hand. Sighing, she forced her way through the words. It was a temporary spell for ease of reading and another for reading quickly. Belinda's shoulders sank in relief, and she smiled gratefully: the spell was a palindrome.

CHAPTER 3

Belinda wore a new-to-her gown down to dinner, as hers weren't ready yet. The slightly used gown swept the floor around her in an elegant train of too-longness and hung loosely about her shoulders and chest. Breathing in deep, quick breaths to keep her chest expanded and the dress up, Belinda walked into the cavernous dining room, fervently praying Beast didn't sigh strongly enough to blow her hair out of position.

Much to the maid's distress, Belinda had taken her hair from its lovely updo to let it hang like a shawl over her shoulders and chest. She'd find what those conniving maids did with the safety pins—and her clothes—before tomorrow if it was the last thing she did.

Beast looked up from the table in surprise as she entered. His intelligent eyes among the soft brown fur of his face was as startling as a blue bird among winter-brown leaves. He continued to stare at her, his surprise evidently freezing him in place, for he didn't rise.

Belinda huffed. He may have forgotten she was there, but she'd make sure he didn't forget his manners completely. An invisible servant pulled out a chair for her across the long table from Beast, but she swished her way down the length of polished wood to stand beside the chair at Beast's side. Cursed or not, the man cared for clothes, for he was dressed for dinner when he apparently expected to eat alone. *The dandy.*

"Good evening, Beast." She smiled demurely at him as he continued to stare at her. *I'm Belinda. Remember me?* "The maids tell me you have an excellent cook. I look forward to gauging his quality for myself." She flicked a glance at the chair and the place setting that quickly appeared at her chosen spot, and continued to smile at Beast.

He cleared his throat and rose to pull back the chair for her. "I am certain you will find him a superior chef, Miss ... ah ... Miss Lambton."

She nodded, impressed, as he pushed the chair in under her. Seated, she attempted to straighten, only to be jerked to a halt. The excess fabric she needed for the top portion of her dress was currently caught under the chair leg. Scooting the chair forward, she yanked on the skirt with one hand and used the other to keep her hair out of the soup.

Cheeks flushing as she successfully sat up, she glanced at Beast, but to her relief, he was glaring at the air beside him, growling something to do with the fragile bowl of soup placed before him. Belinda felt a brush of air on her shoulders as, she imagined, a servant made a hasty exit.

"Beast, dear, might I trouble you for your jacket? It's a little chilly in here. The servants couldn't find a shawl for me earlier when I asked."

Perhaps catching her tone, Beast gave her an examining look before he growled again to the servants, a rather longer growl than before. Belinda smiled smugly as another breeze rushed past her.

"Do you have guests often, Beast? Your family, perhaps?"

"No," he said, draping a pillowcase-sized napkin across his lap. "I *like* to be alone."

"Oh? How agreeable for you. I miss my father. If it weren't for him, I might like to live alone too. Though I do have an aunt who lives a few days' journey away whom I miss on occasion. Loving people adds a bit of pain to life, I find. Life is more pleasant in some ways when you don't care for anyone, don't you think?"

"I didn't say I didn't care for anyone! I—" Beast quieted as a breeze rushed back by. A sturdy mug of soup appeared in front of him, and a pale yellow shawl large enough to wrap Belinda twice floated in and landed delicately over her shoulders. When the servant had left and Beast had said grace, he continued calmly, "Beasts simply prefer to be alone."

"Oh, it's a territorial thing then. So did your parents eat a prince too and get his castle, or did you move up in the world?" Ignoring Beast's glower, Belinda wrapped the shawl over a shoulder, around her chest, and over her other shoulder. "Did they eat an earl or a wealthy merchant?" she continued, tying the shawl in place. *There.* The maid could have a conniption, but Belinda was going to be comfortable.

The mug of soup halfway to his lips, Beast stared at her, as if she were the absurd one of the two. She was only wearing a shawl, he a curse!

"People of wealth and influence," he said at last, then drank his soup in two gulps. Belinda carefully spooned up her own soup and was immensely rewarded when Beast grumbled into his wine goblet a moment later, "And though we don't visit, we keep in touch."

She nodded sweetly at this. "Do give them a greeting from me and a congratulations on raising such a gentlemanly cub."

Beast choked, then lost half his goblet of wine all over the newly served salad. Belinda politely covered the gaff with an,

"Oh! Red wine sauce makes everything better. How clever of you to think of it."

Beast spent the next few minutes coughing and giving her strange looks, which she politely ignored while tucking into her meal, pausing only at the main course, when she noted Beast darting a glance between her and the serving tray–sized haunch of venison and dainty silverware at his place, a hungry, sad look in his eyes.

"Don't mind me," Belinda said cheerily, holding out a speared piece of meat. "I only eat with a fork because I keep my nails cut short. They break if I try to grow them out."

"Thank you ..."

"Don't mention it." She was quiet the rest of the meal, intent on her food and on ignoring the ripping of meat going on beside her.

After the shredding ceased, Beast put aside his napkin and pushed away from the table. Belinda hastily swallowed and called up The Uncurse Plan, Part B: Tampering with Proposals.

"Now, if you'll ex—"

"Join you for a tour of the castle? I'd love to. How kind of you to offer."

"That's not—"

Belinda continued to smile expectantly until his shoulders sank in resignation and he pulled her chair out for her. It was amazing how well smiles worked on him.

"I'm very interested in your library," she said as he offered her his arm.

* * *

THE CRINKLING OF A TURNING PAGE. The pop of a warm fire. The ticktock of a polished grandfather clock. The frantic beating of Belinda's heart as she stood on tiptoe and scanned the shelf of language books. There had to be at least three books on every language on the continent!

She couldn't stuff more than one volume in her shawl and expect Beast not to notice. How was she going to purloin an entire shelf?

They'd finished their brief castle tour and had retired, as per Beast's custom, to the library for the evening. *Retire* was right. He hadn't moved for the past half hour. She itched to be doing *something*. She was almost desperate enough for an embroidery hoop.

The hair on the back of her neck stood up. She glanced over her shoulder to see Beast eyeing her like a mama cat whose kitten was too close to a stranger. Easing back to her heels, she asked, "Do you have a catalogue of your collection?"

"On the desk by the globe."

Glancing around, Belinda spied a neat little desk in a recess of the wall. It held a globe, a handwritten book of titles and their location, a stationery set, a vase of thorns and thistles, and a few broken knickknacks. Belinda adored it. She settled down at it and began writing the titles and locations of the books she needed to hide, then calculated how many books from random places she would need to take to fill in the gaps she was going to make.

Ascertaining that Beast was intent on his book, she rose quietly and casually walked around the giant room—it had twenty-foot-high bookcases and was half the size of her father's house. She slowed near the ladder that ran along a rail on one of the upper shelves and gave it an experimental shove. It slid quietly along the shelf. Hiding a smile, she towed it along toward the language section. She paused one unit before that and plucked out a book with a similar color binding to a few of the language books, then, with a glance at

Beast, inched the ladder over and put her foot on the bottom-most rung.

The hair on the back of her neck stood up. She peeked around her shoulder, then stepped back down. Beast didn't say anything, but she didn't like the way he was looking at her. "What are you reading? I've been having trouble deciding," she said by way of distraction.

He cocked a light, bushy brow at her. "It's a book of fairy tales."

"How entertaining." A strange choice for someone who had no problem *being* cursed. Lessons on how to act like a beast, perhaps? The title read *Exploits and Defeat of the Mysterious Prince Dokar of the Unseelie Faerie*. How to be a villain then. Unlike the "fairy godmother" Lady Violetta, Prince Dokar was a genuine fairy, and as wickedly mischievous as they came, if the tales were true.

Beast didn't reply but seemed to be trying to read the spine of her own book. She glanced down at it: *Trade by Water: Oceans and Rivers and the Laws Pertaining Thereunto.*

Providence must be with her. She held it up for him. "My father was a merchant once. I thought it would be nice to learn more about economics and trade and maybe help get the family business up and going again."

His other eyebrow rose, making a blaze of almond fur across his forehead. "How productive of you," he said, a suspicion in his voice that piqued Belinda's pride.

"My family—that is, my father and I—have that tendency. Father usually goes over the accounts in the evening while I darn socks and shar—" *sharpen the hunting knives* "—listen to him share about his day or what he read in the paper." She continued on, praising her father's diligence and even throwing in for good measure a comment about a recent tariff and the effect of a forecasted storm on the value of shipping goods.

Beast made no response, and his contemplative stare made her uncomfortable. For whatever reason, he seemed a bit more intimidating seated comfortably in that overlarge wingback chair than he had in the forest, more like a bear in his cave. A place he was more likely to defend, she sensed. His ears flattened back like a cat's.

She cleared her throat, deciding that harping on her father's good example was not likely to stimulate Beast to a profitable life in his rightful position.

"Did you learn a trade alongside your father?" she ventured, still standing by the shelf, refusing to give up ground near the language books just yet.

"Yes." He eyed her over the gilded edges of the children's book. "Eating princes." He said it with intentional clarity, his lips pulling back to allow the candlelight to dazzle itself against his razor-sharp teeth.

Drawing back despite herself, she croaked out, "Everyone must have their work, I suppose."

He turned a page, then another, without actually reading them. "Rest and relaxation have their place too, Miss Lambton."

Not for years at a time. Restraining an unladylike huff, Belinda hunted up the leadership section and picked up the most worn volume and sat down with that and *Trade by Water* to make use of the reading spells. The gilded title on the worn cover elicited a double-take as she laid it on the desk. *On Kingly Behavior and the Rights of the People?* Surely he wasn't—

Her nose itched violently, drawing her thoughts away.

If she read enough books, she considered as she wrinkled her nose and tried not to scratch it, and asked enough educated questions, maybe she could stumble on a topic she could engage Beast in. Surely he'd have something to say about whatever area of responsibility he was reared to. If nothing else, he'd hardly let her be more informed than himself and would exert himself to something more than fairytales.

BELINDA HAD a splitting headache when she sneaked back down to the library in the wee hours. It was a pity Lady Violetta hadn't given her an ease of understanding spell to go with the reading spells.

One hand gripping a pillowcase and candle and the other gliding over the banister, she felt her way down the stairs. She wasn't exactly sure why she wanted to make it harder on herself to ignore Beast's forced proposals, but she figured obeying an enchantress was a good idea.

Once in the library, Belinda lit the candle in the low-burning fire, gathered books at random, scurried up the ladder, and began exchanging books and loading the language ones into the pillowcase pressed between her and the ladder.

The steady ticktock of the grandfather clock, the slight chill of the night air, and the crackling of the dying fire eased her headache.

Or perhaps it was the effect of the soft, steady huff of breath against fur.

Belinda froze for six heartbeats, then turned slowly toward the fireplace. She could just see Beast's arm dangling over the side of the enormous chair he was apparently using as a mattress. Was he too lazy even to go up to bed? It wasn't as if he'd done anything useful during the day, that she could tell.

She eased down the ladder, her muscles pleasantly straining with the weight of the loaded pillowcase, and padded across the rug—a rather diseased-looking bear rug—to the door, then jerked to a halt, cursing herself. Beast was bound to want the books she'd purloined to study for his proposals, and when he couldn't find them, he'd set the servants to hunting for them. If they found them in her room, he'd kick her out for sure. Maybe even eat her, as much as he loved to read. But the enchantress had warned her to get them all.

Belinda spied a half-open book on Beast's lap. It wasn't the volume of fairytales.

Curse her. All her curses upon herself!

Belinda set her stash down, then, swallowing hard, shuffled closer to Beast. Stopping about a foot from him, she slowly reached toward his lap. *Don't breathe. Don't make a sound. You'll be fine. Worst case, he'll kick you out the gate to the wolves.* Belinda shivered and pinched the edge of the book cover. It slid smoothly forward over his lap and off. She jerked it up and hurried to put it in her pillowcase, but the firelight caught on an unexpected word: Tactics. Belinda turned the cover toward her and held up the candle. *Naval Tactics of New Grimmland.* She cocked an eyebrow. Was her scheme working already?

Or was it simply something to fall asleep by? It wasn't as if New Beaumont and New Grimmland, though trade competitors, were ever likely to go to war. Come to think of it, hadn't Winthrop mentioned that they were doing some maneuvers together?

Beast shifted, and Belinda darted behind the mate to Beast's enormous chair. He returned to his even breathing. She waited nine heartbeats this time, then crept out and laid the naval book beside Beast's chair, next to a thick envelope. Sneaking a peek at Beast, Belinda picked up the envelope, rubbing her itching nose. She blinked as she struggled to make out the handwriting and seal. The spell must be wearing off, for she couldn't make sense of a thing she read.

Or maybe it was the hour and the returning headache. She could investigate Beast's identity in the morning.

She retrieved her bag and looked around the room again, pausing at the language shelf. What if he did search for the books? Why had she listened to that enchantress? She couldn't even do a proper curse! She—

Belinda's gaze flew back to the little desk she'd claimed. Her lips twisted into a wicked grin. There was more than one way to skin a beast down to his human hide.

CHAPTER 4

B elinda didn't expect to fall asleep quickly in a strange —a very strange—new place, but she did, and she dreamed.

Beast jumped up and down, pushing out a cloud of smoke-like breath into the gray dawn of the castle lawn. Yawning, he jogged in place for a moment before reaching down to touch his toes.

"Good luck this morning, Master." The masculine voice came from a smaller cloud of escaping breath. "Will you be bringing back anyone with you today?" Beast's fur overcoat appeared near the mist, and Beast took it and pulled it on.

"I sincerely hope not, Jenkins," Beast said, shrugging his shoulders to get the fur to hang to his satisfaction. "Right, I'm off."

"We'll have a second breakfast ready as you requested for your return."

"Thank you." Beast set off at a fast walk toward the towering gates.

He loped through a forest that worried Belinda even as she slept. It wasn't her forest.

He slowed as the steeple of a church and the pitched roofs of houses came into view over the treetops. Thin lines of smoke rose into the air.

The unfamiliar town was quiet. Beast sniffed the air appreciatively, as if it were scented with bacon, then stepped boldly within view of the backside of the village as the church bells chimed the hour.

No one turned to stare at him before breaking into yells and running for pitchforks. No one was around. It was breakfast time.

He paced along the perimeter of the forest, darting back into the woods whenever anyone did appear. This continued for a half hour.

"Oh, Beastie! Where are you?"

Beast jumped, his mouth twisting in what likely was an oath.

"Beastie!" the saccharine-coated voice continued.

Beast backed warily toward the trees, his head swiveling back and forth.

"Beastie!" The tone was annoyed.

Beast caught the tone and the direction and took off the opposite way. He zigzagged through the forest. The voice suddenly came from in front of him. Beast darted into a cluster of rhododendrons surrounding a gnarled beech and hunkered behind the leaves.

Light footsteps prowled the path he'd taken, and he shivered. Fur wafted down around him. Some, caught on the breeze, drifted toward the trail. Beast grabbed for the fleeing hair, snagging only as many strands as he shed to the next breeze.

The footsteps stopped, then turned toward the rhododendrons. Beast scooted back, and slid into a hidden hollow, biting his tongue to keep himself quiet as he bounced down. A sizable oak stopped his roll. Scrambling to his knees, Beast scooted around the tree, putting its trunk between him and Saccharine Lady.

"Beast?"

He grabbed a mossy rock from the bank and tossed it up and onto the trail further down. The footsteps moved in that direction. He sat as quietly as a huffing beast could until the faint toll of the church bell sounded three-quarters of an hour. Easing up, he started down the hollow, climbing out parallel to the village but closer to a stream he'd crossed on his way. Picking up his pace, he started off at a lope toward the stream.

"Beast! You'd better wait. I hear you!"

He startled, then with a burst of speed, sprinted the last ten feet and leapt over the stream. The forest beyond wavered. Beast kept running. The gates to the castle shimmered into view.

"Do you want one of these plain, ignorant peasant girls to catch you?" Saccharine Lady's voice floated after him, but somehow, Belinda knew the lady couldn't follow.

Ignorant peasant indeed. Belinda nearly huffed herself awake.

❧❦❧

BELINDA WOKE MID-MORNING, bleary-eyed, tired, and a little confused about why she thought a human voice was coming from empty air and why she was dreaming about a beast with two fur coats.

Oh. She was a guest of a beast with two fur coats.

Embarrassed to be waking so late, she hurriedly dressed in another very fine, very large hand-me-down, wrapped herself up in her shawl, and opened the door. Late though she was, perhaps she had time to chat up the servants and find out who Beast was before he rose.

She stepped out, then lunged back to avoid Beast as he lumbered by, his fur glistening as if he'd just come from a bath.

"Good morning, Miss Lambton." Beast greeted her in a singsong voice, apparently very pleased with himself about something.

Frightening her half out of her wits? Or what wits she had before coffee anyway.

"Wil je met me trouwen?" He stopped to bow slightly, then added, still with that self-satisfied expression, "Just a rhetorical question by way of greeting. A tradition here. No need to answer." His lips spread wide, revealing more teeth than Belinda wished to see in what she fancied was a smile. It was

ghastly. "I'm just going down for a bit of a read before break-fast." He nodded as if in goodbye, then shifted to continue down the hallway.

Belinda blinked. Coffee or no, she couldn't let him outwit her. She pulled up her best obnoxious early morning grin to fortify her and hurried after him. "Why, Beast! How impressive you are. Did you study German—or was that Dutch? I'm never quite sure, but I do believe that was Dutch."

Beast stuttered, then slowly turned back to her. A halo of white rimmed his wide blue irises.

Point for the ignorant peasant.

"I thought you ... um ... didn't know any other languages?"

"Well, *know* and *recognize a few words* are two different things, aren't they?" The white halo grew, taking on a haunted look. "But you didn't answer my question," she continued. "Do you study languages or do you acquire them from those you devour? The latter would be *so* much simpler. I wish I could do it. You know, you inspired me yesterday. I borrowed several language books from the library last night—sleeping in a strange place is always so difficult."

She took Beast's limp arm and led him down the corridor toward the stairs. "I remember seeing that you have a lovely pianoforte. I'm determined to indulge in music while I can and learn to say lovely things like you do. My voice instructor when I was young was a hopeless romantic and forced me to learn a tremendous number of foreign love songs. I think I'll look them up and translate them. What do you think? Will you help me translate? You're so well fed—I mean well-studied."

Beast groaned.

"What was that, Beast?"

"I think I'm going to have a headache."

"Oh dear. Perhaps you'd better go outside. I find fresh air

always helps me. Perhaps a round of archery? Or is that too strenuous for you?"

"I hunt with my teeth," he growled, extricating himself from her and limping down the hallway, "but indulge yourself if you like. Please excuse me."

When Beast was sufficiently far away, Belinda indulged in a snicker and continued on to a shamefully late breakfast.

The fare was more than satisfactory, but the conversation was not. She couldn't get anything out of the servants beyond Beast's love of coffee time, tea time, hot cocoa time, and evening stroll time. She did note, however, that if she crossed her eyes, she could just make out the waver of the servants.

Despite that success, Belinda found the day exceedingly frustrating. Every time she went to the library or tried to find Beast, a servant fetched her for another dress fitting or insisted she go to the kitchen for another dessert. While she was struggling through her fifth donut—a little thing to follow her three slices of cake, two pieces of pie, and cup of gelato—a servant made a whispered comment that it would take a lot of those to get her to the right size.

Right size? To fit those dresses the servants found for her? Groaning, Belinda lowered the last bite of donut back to her plate.

"Eat up, miss!" a cheerful cook's assistant said. "The master will be offended if you don't eat your fill while you're with us."

"How about another cup of tea to help me wash it down?" Belinda asked sweetly.

"Of course, miss."

There was a swish of fabric. Crossing her eyes, Belinda could just tell that the maid had turned away to the pantry.

Belinda darted out of the kitchen, and ran, one hand on her protesting belly, until she found an exit.

Spying a bench outside the stables, she collapsed onto it,

and only with great effort did she manage to keep her insides in their proper place. Moaning, she laid her head back against the stable wall and let the sunshine on the cool day warm her cheeks.

After a few minutes, the noises of people moving about filtered through the wood and windows to her, then voices.

"How is your leg, this morning, Y—"

"*Beast*," hissed a familiar, deep voice. "Call me *Beast*."

Belinda sat up. Beast was *out here?*

The servant, a groom or the stable master Belinda assumed, lowered his voice. "Surely you don't expect the woman to be *out here?*"

Belinda huffed. *She* didn't reportedly spend all her time by a cozy fire.

"Lyndon," he said seriously, "it wouldn't surprise me to find her wherever I am. I'm not certain whether she's cleverer than—than *her*, or just a nuisance. A very strange one, at that."

Belinda gripped a handful of skirt, a familiar pang troubling her heart. It wasn't as if she wanted to fit in with the company of a beast content to be cursed! Here, it was a good thing to be "strange."

"Why did you allow her to come?" Lyndon asked.

"Because, well … well, you know what happened the last time I ignored someone 'in need.'"

"What kind of 'in need' is this one?"

"Oh, she gave some tale about her father being gone and some villager pestering her." He added in a mutter, "She had such a desperate look in those big brown eyes of hers that I believed her."

"Rather pretty, is she?"

"I'm not interested," Beast growled.

I should hope not!

"I should hope not," the servant continued, amused, "if

she's a strange village lass. You never were one to let a pretty face ruin your reason. I'm glad that hasn't changed."

There was a pause before Beast asked, concern in his tone, "Is Robert still crazy about Lucrezia?"

"Yes," Lyndon said with a sneer. "I can't understand it. He used to be almost as wise as you in terms of reading people. But now? He's either seemingly trying to avoid the woman, or it's 'Yes, Lucrezia. Whatever you say, Lucrezia.'" His toned changed. "It worries me."

Beast didn't reply, and Belinda wished she could see if his face expressed concern. If it was even capable of such a mien.

"But your leg ... Master Beast?" Lyndon asked a moment later.

"It's a little stiff this morning. It will limber up as we walk, I'm sure."

"Ah. I haven't noticed it bothering you since——"

"I know," said Beast, his tone worried.

"Perhaps," Lyndon said hesitantly, "perhaps, this is a good thing. If——"

"How could this possibly be a good thing?" Beast snarled.

"Master——"

"It's better this way."

The wind stirred the dry leaves in the trees at the stable's edge before Lyndon replied, sadly, "You play a dangerous game, my lord."

Game? Belinda shivered along with leaves in the silence that followed.

"It's better this way." Beast's voice wasn't so confident as before. "Come, Lyndon. To the woods."

Belinda groaned. Of course they'd come out her way. She started to rise but sank back to the bench when her stomach bucked her lead.

Inside, voices gave way to footsteps, one set much heavier than the other.

Leaning her head against the stable wall, Belinda closed her eyes and relaxed.

"Where shall we go today?" The servant's voice was resigned.

"The southern section. I ..." Beast sighed. His heavy footfalls stopped. A second set of soft ones retreated to the stable. The light beyond Belinda's eyelids darkened and a claw poked her shoulder.

"Hey!" Belinda cried, opening her eyes and clutching her shoulder to wipe away the strange sensation and make sure she wasn't punctured. "What do you think you're doing?"

"You were drooling."

"I was not!"

Beast cocked an eyebrow at her. "Go to your room to sleep."

Belinda leaned back against the wall and crossed her arms, then moved them to her side when her stomach protested the extra weight. "I will not. I came out here to escape. Your servants are trying to force feed me, to fatten me up or some such nonsense."

"Are they? How delicious—for you, I mean."

Belinda glared at him. He had that cunning look about him again.

She smiled sweetly and rose carefully. "Might I walk with you? I feel in need of exercise."

"I'm not going for a walk. Go inside and take a nap."

"But I promised to help you with—"

He leaned closer, the cunning look shifting suddenly to one of command. "Go inside." He said it in that way that showed his teeth very well.

Who was she to gainsay the request of her host?

"As you wish, Beast." Belinda curtsied and walked slowly back toward the front of the castle, the hair on the back of her neck giving her the impression Beast was watching.

She was met at the door by a floating tray.

"Miss Lambton! We just made fresh batches of all Beast's favorite cookies. Won't you taste test them for us? We made hot cocoa to go with them!"

Belinda took a nap in self-defense.

⚜

BELINDA WAS able to descend to dinner in a dress that fit—temporarily, if she listened to the servants' not-quite-whispered comments about getting her fattened up and needing her gowns let out by the next week. Beyond that, she wouldn't need them any more, they whispered in a knowing manner.

"Isn't the lamb superb?" Beast said solicitously halfway through the main course. All attempts at conversation on her part had been redirected to food and encouragements for her to eat until she'd given up and just eaten. Her portions at dinner were twice as large as they had been the evening before.

Belinda managed half a smile. "Excellent."

"Eat up." Beast's broad, toothy grin was a trifle too wide.

Sighing, Belinda put down her fork and pulled out a small glass bottle she'd purloined from the healer's room earlier. If she were destined to be strange, she was going to be successful at it. And she'd use that trait to help a certain recalcitrant, cursed beast, since doing so meant helping her father.

She ran her thumb over the bottle's cork stopper. It was time to enact The Uncurse Plan, Part C: Preventing Run-off Belinda Attempts. She'd managed an hour in the library before dressing for dinner and had made good use of it.

She removed the cork from the bottle and drank the water she'd filled it with. Giving an exaggerated shiver, she replaced the cork. For good measure, she gave a genteel cough and patted her chest, repeating that until Beast looked fully her way.

"Um ... Miss Lambton, are you ill?"

"Me?" *Genteel cough and chest pat.* "Oh no. I am always in perfect health. Thank you."

"But you just—"

"Oh this!" She held up the bottle. "This is my daily dose of Mithridatium."

Beast's eyes took on a bluebird-before-a-sky-of-white-clouds look. "Mithridatium?" he repeated questioningly, the tone more of shock at her than an unfamiliarity with the elixir.

"Yes, the universal poison antidote." She pulled out another small bottle, this one filled with powdered sugar saved from the pastries sent up to her room as an appetizer. "Which reminds me." She tapped the powder into her mouth and swallowed, making a face fit for unsweetened lemonade. After putting the bottle away, she daintily wiped her lips, hoping her cheeks weren't as red as they felt.

He gaped at her.

"When I was young," she continued after a sip of wine, "we had a neighbor who died under *suspicious* circumstances. My father was reading to us at the time about the great king of Pontus, King Mithridate, about his fear of being poisoned and thus his habit of ingesting small doses of poison to build an immunity, and his invention of the Mithridatium elixir. I determined I would never be poisoned, so I take my daily doses."

She flicked a knowing glance his way. "I pity any wild creature who might think to make a meal of me, what with my daily doses and all. I'm quite poisonous by now but unharmed thanks to the elixir."

Beast didn't respond. He was still gaping.

Putting aside her napkin, she leaned back in the chair.

"I've had enough to eat tonight, excellent meal though it was. I wouldn't want to be *fattened up* like a lamb for slaughter, especially not after your servants so kindly made me this lovely dress. You won't be offended by my not eating dessert, will you, Beast?"

Beast closed his mouth, then cleared his throat under Belinda's placid smile. "No, not at all."

"You're very kind. As I recall, Mithridate was a formidable general as well as a king. If you were a military man, Beast, what would be your opinion of the recent naval maneuvers? I noticed you get the papers; you must have read about them."

His eyes returned to their bluebirds-in-the-clouds look before narrowing in what might have been anger. "I only read the comics."

"Do you?"

"Yes," Beast said coldly. "Are you well versed in poisons, Miss Lambton?"

"Only enough to ensure my own safety."

His eyes narrowed even more, as if in suspicion, though of what she had no idea. He put his napkin beside his half-full plate and rose. "If you'll excuse me?" he said, an actual anger, not mere irritation, in his tone.

Gaping herself now, Belinda stared after him as he stormed out, bellowing to the servants about him going to the tower and not wanting to be disturbed.

When the door closed in what might be a polite slam, Belinda leaned her elbow on the table and rubbed her forehead. So far she'd managed to make a fool and a nuisance of herself.

With a sad laugh she threw her bottles into the fire. She was as bad at this uncurse business as the enchantress. *What do I have to do? Can you even force someone into a change of heart?*

And if he did release his curse, would he allow Belinda to stay until her father returned?

CHAPTER 5

Belinda woke shortly after dawn with a headache and a terrible restless feeling. She hadn't dreamed of Beast but of Gaspard. He was hunting for her and was concerned. Aside from the pastor and his wife, and a few older ladies, Gaspard was the only one to care for her, and certainly the only one her age to want her around. He and his uncle had been the ones to teach her to hunt and fish, skills that had greatly helped her family, as he'd often reminded her. Was she wrong to run from him? Would love grow in time if she married him?

Groaning, Belinda rolled out of bed. It was more than a lack of romantic love that made her reject Gaspard. It was a lack of character on his part. She wasn't going to let her current mood steal her future. Nor a curse. She was not the type to give in to gray. She just needed something to do, hands-on.

Belinda dressed, tidied the already clean room, then went in search of the seamstress, who promptly barred her from helping with the dressmaking. She was afraid to go near the kitchen. She ventured to the library, only to find it empty.

After re-reading her spells, she set herself the goal of an hour of study. Within a quarter-hour, however, she began to nod. She fell asleep wondering how someone who never napped could nap twice in two days.

The morning mist seeping through the forest swirled about Beast as he strolled, seeming neither too bashful to cling to him nor bold enough to shroud him entirely. He didn't let this uncertainty bother him but marched along as if familiar with the path, even as Belinda struggled to force the scene into a recognizable one. But she couldn't. Why did she always dream of new places yet the same Beast and saccharine-voiced huntress? Why did it worry her that she didn't recognize the forest beyond the dream gate?

Beast slowed as the woodland broke suddenly for a worn wagon trail. Muffled sounds from around a bend caught his attention. He listened, ears perked, then crept along the edge of the dirt road and peered around the curve darkened by thick trees and shrubs. A low growl erupted from his throat.

Four men, faces concealed by handkerchiefs, unloaded crates from a man's wagon laden with market-day goods. A fifth man, armed with a cocked pistol, reminded the merchant of the benefits of not protesting such treatment.

Another growl low in Beast's throat caused the bandits to look around nervously. Beast crouched, as if about to spring, then shuddered as he looked down at his claws. Squaring his shoulders, he used his paw to swirl the mist about him, as if asking it to cloak him, and picked up a sturdy branch.

The gunman cried out and dropped his weapon as a knife buried itself in his shoulder.

"Unhand his belongings, cowards!" A man in his mid- to late-twenties with a military bearing, scarred face, and worn traveling clothes burst from the mist and tackled one bandit. "Get the gun, merchant," he yelled as he leapt up, leaving the bandit unconscious. He quickly engaged another in a very short round of fisticuffs, which left that bandit insensible as well.

*Beast stared, then shook himself with a sigh and backed into the
woods. He watched quietly, shoulders drooped, for the few minutes it
took for the newcomer and the merchant to subdue and tie up the
bandits, then toss them into the back of the wagon. Beast turned away
and trudged back around the curve and across the road into the forest
beyond. A branch snapped under his heavy tread just as the trees and
mist concealed him.*

*The newcomer looked up, then darted into the woods. "Rupert!" he
cried, searching in vain to see through the mist and trees. "Rupert!
Quit being a bloody idiot and come out!"*

*Wasn't Rupert the prince's name? Belinda's nose itched, very real-
istically for a dream, and she promptly forgot something important
she'd been thinking.*

*The mist continued to cloak Beast until he neared the back of the
village. There, it thinned and roamed away to the village square, as if
drawn to it by the noises of market day. Beast paced, slower than
usual, until a light footstep disturbed the forest. He sniffed the air and
took off running. An irritated, feminine cry of "Beast!" followed.*

Belinda woke with a start, blinking against candlelight and
filtered sunlight, and rubbed at the indentation in her forehead that bore remarkable resemblance to the edge of a book.

"You know they make beds for napping?"

Rather than glare at Beast, who was standing beside her
examining the books before her, Belinda's hand shot out to
cover her book-pillow, praying she'd not drooled on it.
Turning slightly from him, she shook her head to clear away
the last tendrils of sleep. "You can't tell me *you've* never slept
in your chair."

"I wouldn't dream of denying it, but my chair is comfortable." As if to prove it, he eased down into the crimson cushions with a contented sigh. "You've been hunched over a
desk."

"Have you been watching me sleep?" Belinda demanded,
facing him. She was surprised by a faint glow about him, as

he'd had the prior morning. It was almost like the glow of exercise. There was amusement in his eyes as he met her gaze.

"Only from the doorway here."

"Where have you been this morning?" she asked, narrowing her eyes.

He arched an eyebrow to indicate that was a foolish question, then picked up a collection of plays. "I take my sleep very seriously."

"And I take my—" *work very seriously*. She had no work here and didn't want to give Beast an opening to get rid of her by implying she had duties to return to.

"Daily doses very seriously?" he added wryly before Belinda could come up with an alternate reply.

That piqued. "My promise to help you in exchange for you sheltering me. What can I do for you?"

"For me, nothing. But feel free to be an idle, demanding mistress to my servants until your father returns. Unaccountably, they seem to enjoy work, and having someone else to do things for pleases them. So enjoy yourself for the remainder of your stay." He waved his arm to indicate the entirety of the castle. "You have at your disposal all the spoils of the dearly departed prince's estate: a fine forest and pleasure gardens, archery equipment, stable, billiard rooms, music room, books, and ... fine foods. Ah," he exclaimed, observing the full breakfast tray floating through the doorway to him. "This beats breakfast in bed."

Resisting the urge to roll her eyes, Belinda grabbed a book on economics and left. Beast may have conceded she'd beat him at his little game of scaring her into believing she was to one day be dinner, but naps made her cranky. And she had no desire to hear Beast eat more than once a day.

As she skirted the kitchen in favor of a safer exit, Belinda analyzed her dream. Beast could have helped but didn't. Like the enchantress said, he preferred to stay comfortable and let others do what he should do. But what could *she* do about it?

There was a nip in the air outside, but Belinda didn't mind the cold so long as she had sunshine. She found the bench outside the stable again and settled down to read. A third of the way through the book, the brush of wood as the stable door shut startled her out of the pages. As she looked up, lines of letters magically clear to her were replaced by a precisely pressed, somewhat frilly, extravagantly blue servant's garb on a middle-aged man. Her nose itched as she squinted at the unexpected outfit.

The man stopped short just outside the stable door, his gaze colliding with hers in an expression of shock and alarm. Recovering quickly, he smiled at her and made as if to keep moving.

"You're visible. Why are you visible?" Belinda demanded, gaping at him, inexplicably concerned lest an intruder had invaded Beast's sanctuary and meant to harm him.

Her question drew him to a halt, and he faced her fully. "Why are you?"

"I wasn't cur—"

He gave a half-smile at her abandoned answer. "Very wise of you, Miss Lambton." He motioned to the seat beside her. "It's not something we should talk about."

Belinda shut her mouth and scooted over for him to sit.

"I'm Lyndon," he said, but she'd already guessed that. He was Beast's confidante. Now that she saw him, she judged him a personal servant or valet rather than a stable master. Was he not here at the time of the curse? Or was he saved from it to be the method of communication with Beast's family?

"It's a pleasure to meet you." Belinda nodded, her closer examination of him failing to move past his face. He had a kind, weather beaten one, with a touch of white about the temples, and something fatherly and stately in his eyes that made her heart ache for her own father.

"You never thought the sight of a face, even a stranger's, could be comforting, did you?" he asked, amused.

Blushing, Belinda looked away. "No. I generally only expect my father's to have that effect." But then, she'd never expected to go for a long time without seeing another human face.

"How long before he returns?"

"Another six weeks, if all goes well."

"What will you do when he returns?"

"Run home as fast as I can." She added quietly, "I don't like being an annoying interloper." Especially an unsuccessful one.

Lyndon laughed. "I'm glad it's not your true personality. So what can I do for you, Miss Lambton? You should know, however, that I don't give information."

"I didn't come for favors, merely to be outside."

"There's nothing you'd like to do more than read outside then?" he said skeptically.

"I'd rather be doing something active, if only I knew what." Her eyes brightened with an idea. "I'd love to go for a hunt. I provided meat for my family; I could provide some here. I'd like to do something useful. I'm not accustomed to being a guest."

Would her modeling a life of useful, cheerful activity spur Beast to noble deeds of the same where tales hadn't? A mental image of Beast lounging in his well-worn wingback chair, looking like a natural part of it, flitted through her thoughts. She gave her head a slight shake.

"To let others do for you is, at times, a good thing, Miss Lambton," Lyndon said, with an almost scolding tone. "Good for you and good for others." He motioned toward the stable. "We have someone who hunts for us. How about a ride? I managed to save your clothes for you, so you could wander the grounds in greater comfort and"—he eyed her trailing gown—"safety."

"Thank you," she said with feeling. "I would like a ride."

"Excellent. Come along. You can change inside." Lyndon rose, and she followed along behind him to the stable door. She stopped just short of it.

"Wait. The horses weren't turned into dragons or snakes as part of the curse, were they?"

Lyndon chuckled, his eyes widening dramatically as he answered, "Elephant-sized cockroaches."

She gave an exaggerated shiver. "Well, in that case ... lead on."

He obeyed, guiding her between the rows of stalls to the staircase leading to the rooms above.

"Are you sleeping out here because of me?" she asked with chagrin as she spotted saddlebags thrown over a stall door.

"Beast didn't want me to give away his secrets, and it's no trouble. I'm only here for a few days."

"Well, his secret is out, so you might as well go in where it's more comfortable."

Lyndon nearly ran into a stall door. "*All* his secrets?" he asked, staring back at her.

"Well, no," Belinda admitted, taken aback by his concern. "Just the big one—he's not a convincing beast. As to other secrets, it would no doubt be interesting to discover them, but as they don't directly concern me, I shan't pry."

"You don't know who he is then?"

"No, and that does concern me, so I'm not above snooping to figure that out. However," she said, squinting and giving his outfit a sideways glance, which made her nose itch, "I have a distinct feeling someone—besides Beast—doesn't want me to know, and that one has unusual methods to prevent me from discovering it." Or perhaps the enchantress merely wanted to tease Belinda, but either way, it was annoying.

"Why is that?"

"You're not wearing a very starched, very flamboyant formal blue suit, are you?"

He glanced down at his chest, confused. "No, I'm—ah, wearing something that might give Beast away."

Belinda thought so. *Meddling enchantress.* "You won't tell me what it is?"

"No," he answered emphatically, leaving her at the door to a small room, which he entered. He picked up a paper-wrapped bundle from atop a small trunk, then returned to her. "You may change here while I see about a horse for you." He and Belinda exchanged places, and Belinda closed the door between them. Above the crinkling of paper as she unwrapped her clothes, she heard him walk away. Even his gait reminded her of her father.

"Wait, Mr. Lyndon," Belinda called through the wooden door.

The footsteps stilled. "Yes, Miss Lambton?"

"Do you know how to bring about a change of heart?"

There was a sharp gasp, then a heavy pause, and Belinda feared she'd asked too much. But she had no one else to go to for wisdom.

"That's a fluid term, Miss Lambton," he answered at last, his tone heavy, making her wonder if he'd tried and failed in the same endeavor himself. "It depends on the heart and what is required of it. If the heart lacks whatever it is all together, then naught save a miracle could plant it there and make it flourish. But if whatever it is *is* there, like a blazing fire burned low or a tree cut to the roots, it will require careful tending to flourish again." He added so softly, and sadly, Belinda almost didn't catch the words, "And the desire to change. A hope that it's for the best. And that requires a miracle too."

Belinda paused, one boot on, the other in her hand. "A tree cut down, Mr. Lyndon? Or a buried sprout?" Was Beast ever more than the talking blanket he was now?

"I said 'tree,' but perhaps a buried sprout works as well, as it can grow from a tree stump as readily as from a seed. Why?"

"It's a useful thing to know, don't you think?"

"Yes," he said after a pause. "Allow me to recommend, however, that this endeavor of yours begin with an effort to make sure what you seek is there to begin with. I'll meet you downstairs."

৩✺৩

THE HORSEBACK RIDE, like the indulgent bath, reminded Belinda of her life prior to her father's financial ruin. Unlike her older sisters, she *could* do without such fine things, but she still wished her father back doing what he loved as a successful merchant—maybe then her sisters, both married and living far away, would stop ignoring him. And if his success and happiness meant she could have such nice things again, she wouldn't complain. She would also be free of Gaspard. Which was another reason to figure out Beast and get him uncursed.

Aside from running through futile ideas in that direction, Belinda found the ride exhilarating and the woods about the castle grounds enchanting rather than enchanted. She spotted several wild plants that reminded her of those she'd collected to sell to the healer in her village, and determined to speak with the castle's healer the next day to see if she needed the plants.

Wild herbs are unobtrusive. The thought struck her forcibly as she turned her horse's head for the castle. *That's part of what makes finding them so delightful.* She lifted her fingers to her nose, enjoying the lingering fragrance of a wild mint she'd found and rubbed to release its aroma. She'd been too obtrusive and—if she admitted it—obnoxious in her efforts to free Beast. Quietness and subtlety were more likely to work upon a studious and silent creature like him.

He might be a tiny sprout and merely that, or all that remained of a once mighty tree, for he had kindly let her stay as a guest rather than a servant. Perhaps she just needed to clear the way for the sprout to grow. Too much fertilizer killed, after all.

AFTER DINNER, Beast challenged Belinda and Lyndon to a game of riddles, during which Belinda was strategically dense during a covert proposal, unintentionally dense at other times, and remarkably shrewd, even if she did say so herself, at others. She noticed Beast's frustration with her cunning almost-understanding of his cloaked proposal with something akin to shame, but she didn't wish to gainsay an enchantress and make proposals easy on him, even if she did plan to be less obnoxious in other ways.

And she couldn't help being clever enough to figure out the majority of his riddles.

CHAPTER 6

W hatever spell on the castle that kept her forcibly
abed late some mornings, or sent her into
sudden slumber during the day, did its work on
Belinda the next morning. Unable to stop it, her dream
followed Beast's vigil near another unknown village, the
terrain around it strangely flat compared to her home. No one
saw him. Except the Lady of the Saccharine Voice.

Belinda awoke to a drizzling morning, the gray of it
seeping into her bones, making the castle even more friend-
less than usual. A dangerous emptiness settled in her chest.
She would *almost* have wished even for Gaspard's greeting as
she left her room. That thought caused her to stiffen her
spine and go in search of amusement.

She played the piano for a while, then sought the
warmth and brightness of the library fire. Perhaps, if she
dared admit it, the visible company of an overgrown blanket
dressed in fine velvet. Even his mild version of life would be
something.

But Beast treated her with polite indifference, barely
remarking even on her presence. Belinda bore it quietly for

the sake of The Uncurse Plan, Part D: Don't Over Fertilize, and the sake of her pride.

❀

THE NEXT FEW days continued much the same, gray without and gray within. The Lady of the Saccharine Voice was now a common presence in her dreams, and Gaspard and her father haunted her thoughts as Belinda grew wearier and wearier of the quietness of the castle. Even the novelty of her reading spells was wearing off. The grayness buffeted her.

But a Lambton didn't give up, and certainly didn't give in, she reminded herself as often as she needed to, which was often.

❀

"I WILL NOT GIVE in to gray," Belinda whispered to herself, raised her chin, and marched into the library, now a familiar space after a week's residence at the castle. Per custom, Beast was settled in his cozy chair. After a brief greeting, Belinda, eschewing scholarly "Uncurse Plan" books for the time being, chose a biography of a famed explorer, one she'd heard her father mention as an entertaining read, and nestled into a comfortable chair she'd had her eye on rather than sitting primly at the desk she normally claimed.

She sensed Beast glance at her curiously several times before he finally asked, "What are you reading, Miss Lambton? Nothing so studious as to require a desk and paper?"

A grin twisted her mouth, half of relief and half of amused gratitude. "Don't over fertilize" apparently required days of silence and an adventure book. She considered implying she was plotting something, but she decided to forgo the pleasure. Instead, she merely raised the book to let him read the title, quietly re-arranging her yellow shawl over her shoulders with her free hand as he read.

"Ah," he said, recognition in his tone.

"It's something I hope will be a pleasurable experience. My father once recommended it."

Beast nodded, and returned his interest to his own book. "He has good taste."

"I've always thought so," Belinda replied, and let the room lapse into silence. She didn't speak again for some time, not even to goad Beast when he swapped the collection of plays for another book, one she couldn't catch the title of without him noticing her attempt to do so. The dullness of the cover indicated a work of a serious nature, which surprised her, but she couldn't confirm it.

Lyndon joined them for dinner, and they played a game of riddles, Belinda very nearly, but not quite, understanding Beast's proposal. When they returned to their books later that evening, each supplied with a hot chocolate, Belinda quietly took up the explorer's biography again. An hour later, she was surprised when Beast, with genuine curiosity in his tone rather than mere politeness, asked her what she thought of it. She was even more surprised when her answer, the kind her father enjoyed but made her sisters roll their eyes, led to a short, but satisfying, discussion of it.

❧

THE SKIES CLEARED mid-morning the next day, and Belinda, having learned the healer had no need of her herbs at present, decided to go for a ride and map the location of the wild plants she found for future reference. The healer assured her such a map might come in handy.

The smell of forest and the rustling of leaves soothed

Belinda's soul as she led Marigold through a break in the steep bank to reach the stream whose rush of water she'd been following for some quarter of an hour. That the stream was near the border of Beast's lands she knew, though how she knew, she wasn't sure, nor did she care to concern herself with the how of it. What she did know was she should have asked Lyndon for a proper map to record her findings on, rather than attempting to draw her own, but she hadn't seen him that morning.

As Marigold drank at the stream's rock-and-sand edge, Belinda studied the stream, as she did every body of water. Having her father lose his fortune—and crews she'd never known and now never could—to shipping disasters had given her a respect and fear of the sparkling, alluring sustainer and taker of life.

This was an ordinary, pretty stream, likely crossable by wagon at this particular spot in the dry season. Large boulders, clothed in flat, gray-and-white lichen, sat serenely in the channel a little farther down, not caring how they diverted the flow and made eddies in the water. Belinda wasn't sure whether to admire their tenacity in the face of such roaring onslaught or pity them, knowing how the water would wear them down eventually. She felt the danger of that wear in her own soul: *Go home and marry Gaspard. You know you will eventually, so go ahead. Do you think you deserve someone better? That someone better would want you?*

Gritting her teeth, Belinda picked up a pebble and hurled it at the largest boulder. It hit with a sharp thwack and plummeted to the stream. The boulder remained, unmoved. She threw another pebble, then another, and another, each hit echoing more loudly than the last.

She stopped, panting slightly, and rubbed her aching arm. *That's* what she thought about such gray thoughts. They were as useless as they were foolish.

Returning to the bank, she leaned into the crook of a tree that had grown parallel to the ground for a few feet before it remembered it was supposed to chase the sun, and pulled out her map. She marked the stream's course and the plants she spotted along its bank. That done, she took up her mare's reins again, but the soreness of her thighs convinced her that walking was a good thing to add to her outing.

"Come along, Marigold." Belinda led them back through the gap in the bank and onto the flat floodplain beyond it. "Let's see how many species we can find before another storm sends us to the castle."

"I wish you could tell me," she said a few minutes later, stopping to mark a clump of ginseng on her map, "who Beast is. Every time I think I figure it out, my nose itches and I forget. That bloody enchantress could have at least used a more dignified means of distraction, a spasm of the little toe or some such thing. I could do something about that with no one noticing."

The horse whinnied and shook her head, sending a fly away from her golden mane.

Belinda shooed it with her hand and noted a patch of blackberry canes topping a rise in the bank just ahead to her right. "You're not telling me you're really a servant, are you? Or that dealing with a spasm of the hoof would *not* be less dignified than scratching your nose?"

The horse snorted and pricked her ears toward the rise. Belinda quickly glanced around, but when she didn't see or hear anything to cause her alarm, she dismissed Marigold's nervousness as her imagination. Marigold pranced as they started forward. "All right. No questions about the master. I know that—"

The hair on the back of her neck stood as limbs snapped ahead of them. A buck burst from the shrubs and trees, a broken arrow in its chest. Its crazed eyes found them just before it charged.

The mare reared and darted to the bank's edge, dragging Belinda with her, until Belinda's foot caught in the hole of a decayed tree. Screaming, she tumbled to the forest floor, her arm catching on the toothy stub of beaver-ravaged sapling as Marigold charged on. The sapling ripped through her sleeve, gashing her arm, as blackberry canes clung jealousy to her skirt.

The buck stumbled and collapsed a few feet to her left. It rocked its massive head and shoulders up, struggling to get its legs underneath it, but each jerking movement only shifted it closer to where Belinda raced to free her skirt. The buck reared and collapsed a final time. Belinda shrieked as its antlers hammered her legs into the leaves and wild gingers. She scrambled forward, desperate to escape the dead thing, rough bone and thorns gouging her legs. What had she been thinking, going into woods she knew were hunted without telling anyone!

From just over the ridge where her horse had fled, came an equine cry that chilled her blood. The mare burst back over the rise. Belinda scrambled backwards and covered her head as the mare leapt over both her and the deer. The ground trembled as she landed, faltered, then galloped away.

Only the tremble of the ground under heavy footfalls didn't end when the mare vanished among the trees. Over the bank, limbs snapped and air ruffled through a large snout. A bear nearly as large as the mare, hunkering on all fours and moving fast in its bow-legged fashion, lumbered over the bank. It drew up, standing at the top of the ridge, and sniffed. Its gaze switched from the horse's path to the bloody patch that was Belinda and the deer, then surged toward them, all fur and fang and muscle.

Knowing her voice was her only true weapon, Belinda

screamed, scattering dirt and leaves as she scooted further under the deer's rack and grabbed for the little, useless knife in her belt.

A blur of soft blue velvet and coarse fur sailed over her head and collided into the bear in a blend of roars that were all animal. Beast and bear tumbled over the bank.

"Beast!" The rough weight of bone and deer dug into Belinda's leg and back as she fought to pull her knees underneath her. But the ground was slick with moist leaves and blood, and the deer was heavy. She collapsed, gaining a scrape along her side to match that on her legs. Her cry of pain and frustration echoed a fiercer one along the stream. She had the horrible idea it should have been a man's yell but wasn't. Unable to move, she buried her head under her arms, desperate to block out the snarls and yelps from over the ridge, both horrified and grateful the dominant roar had a familiar edge to it.

"Miss Lambton! Hurry!" The call came to her attention as the weight of the antlers eased off her back and legs. Lyndon grunted as he heaved the buck to the side by its massive rack. As his hands circled about her waist, Belinda managed to uncover her head. With him pulling more than assisting, she staggered to her feet.

With a crunch and a cry that made Belinda sick, the fight over the ridge went silent. Lyndon steadied Belinda, then darted toward that lack of sound. Belinda ran, swaying, after him, topping the rise just behind him.

"Master! Are you all right?" Lyndon cried. Belinda grabbed his arm to keep herself from falling down the bank.

Unhearing, Beast rolled away from the bear's broken carcass, spitting out blood and chunks of fur and flesh. He scrambled back and frantically wiped his mouth over his sleeve, smearing blood rather than getting it off. With a guttural cry, he ripped his jacket and waistcoat off, yanked off his partly unsoiled shirt, and scrubbed it over his face and paws.

"Beast! Are you okay?" It was a fool's question she knew, but she couldn't help herself.

Beast hunched over, shifting on his knees until his back was to them. "Get her away, Lyndon." His rumbly voice cracked.

Lyndon grabbed Belinda by the shoulders and spun her around.

"But, Beast—?"

"Get her away!"

Lyndon dragged Belinda back over the bank, stopping some twenty feet away to bandage the gash on her arm with his handkerchief, then helped her limp through the woods until they found Marigold caught in a thorn patch. They rode back to the castle in grim silence. There, he handed her off to the servants and hurried back to the forest.

Sometime later, Belinda heard a commotion in the corridor outside her room, but invisible hands wouldn't let her up from her bed. Exhaustion, blood loss, and, she suspected, medicine soon sent her to sleep.

She dreamed Beast came and inquired about her, a bandage about his hand and angry welts on his arms and neck. When the servants told him she would be fine so long as the fever didn't linger long, he sent everyone but Lyndon from her room. She wanted to speak, to ask if he was truly well, to tell him how sorry she was, how grateful she was, but she couldn't get her mouth to work with her thoughts. She couldn't get her eyes to open enough to show that she knew he was there.

"Belinda Lambton, will you marry me, a beast?" he asked coldly, then left.

She hadn't even thanked him.

As the day turned into night, the dreams shifted, growing

more disoriented and wild, becoming twisted versions of things she didn't want to remember at all, sounds that made her stomach churn, sights that made her heart quake. She woke in the wee hours, feverish and sweating, and curled in on herself, her thoughts churning and tossing her like a boat in a typhoon.

She'd nearly been killed by a bear.

Beast had saved her.

He'd nearly died, and it had been her fault.

Beast had saved her.

He'd had to act the animal he appeared to be, and for that, he'd never forgive her.

It was all her fault.

He'd nearly died. For her.

Dreams warped by fever took her again until the cool mist of dawn, a swirling vapor about Beast as he walked the forest path past the gates, calmed her. He didn't look particularly heroic, but looks could be deceiving, she decided. But did heroes forgive? She'd done nothing but wrong him.

She woke as Beast cleared the gate a second time, an angry, saccharine-coated warning following him.

CHAPTER 7

T he fever eased to mild warmth by dinner the next day. That and her pleading gained her permission to go downstairs. Gray was in her bones, and she felt in need of color. Was Beast as well as the servants claimed? Why hadn't she thought to let Beast and Lyndon know she would be out in the woods, where they might be hunting?

It was a slow journey to the dining room, her legs and back scraped raw and bandaged and a jagged cut on her arm sewn and wrapped.

The room was empty when she reached it. A waver in the air followed her in and pulled a chair back for her. She sat gingerly and waited.

And waited. She'd left nothing behind upstairs, she admitted to herself shortly, simply given her pain and thoughts a different background; a different tone of *ticktock, ticktock*; a different rhythm of wood popping in a different fire. All still gray.

Was he all right? Would he come down? Would he forgive her?

The fringe of her shawl was beginning to fray from her

twisting of it when the clock struck the quarter-hour. Belinda jumped, and the door opened.

He'd nearly died for her.

"Beast!" she cried in greeting, rising from her chair.

"Forgive me for keeping you waiting, Miss Lambton." Beast's cold reply as he walked in beside Lyndon settled Belinda back into her chair as if blown into it by an icy wind.

"There's nothing to forgive," she stammered. "I was concerned you were unwell."

"Beasts heal quickly and fully." There was a strange edge to his voice, and a glance from Lyndon, that gave the boast some additional meaning she couldn't decipher. Beast seated himself and spread his napkin across his lap before looking back at her. "And you, Miss Lambton, how are you? I hear your fever is better."

"Yes, it is. I am merely ... tired and in some pain, but it's not bad, not like it could have been. I want—"

"I'm glad your fever is better." There was an obvious finality in his tone, an icy wind again.

Belinda blinked rapidly and shut her mouth. She was right. He'd never forgive her. *She'd* never convince him to change, never help her father by it and free herself of Gaspard in the process. If he wished to remain as he was, who was she to interfere anyway?

At least, she thought sadly as the wavers in the air backed away from the table, leaving a steaming bowl of soup for her, she knew one thing about Beast: he was not the type who did things "freely," yet always reminded her of what she owed. She had no need to fear there.

"Beast," she said softly. "I've troubled you enough. You've been a generous host, but I will go home tomorrow."

"You can't."

Belinda blinked, and in that blink, a hint of the fire's red glow drove away some of the gray. "Why not?" she said sharply.

"As of yesterday, it would be a very long trip."

Yesterday? "What do you mean?" An unpleasant conclusion wove itself together in her mind. She expected her nose to itch, but it didn't. Her throat tightened instead.

"The village outside the castle shifts daily. The cycle will not return to your village until six weeks from the day you joined us. You're currently across the kingdom, and neither I nor my servants can accompany you to keep you safe."

Shock strangled the gray chill, and she wasn't sure whether it was relief or horror, or both, that wove together to form its strong fingers.

"I warned you not to come."

"I remember." She fumbled for her spoon with her left hand, her injured right tucked against her chest. Why had she trusted him enough to follow him in the first place? Had she been so desperate?

"When your village returns, I will send you home to your father."

"And if he's not there?" Lyndon asked, a paternal concern to his voice that brought the ever-present ache of her heart to the surface.

Beast said nothing.

Lyndon frowned at him, then sent Belinda a look telling her to stay as long as needed.

She returned a sad, noncommittal smile, and feigned focus on her meal. She stirred her soup awkwardly, paying little attention to it as she lifted the broth-filled spoon to her mouth, then fished around the bowl absently for another spoonful.

What's your choice now, Belinda, if he doesn't return on time, or ever? A lonely castle with a Beast who despised her presence or a father-less home with an unrelenting Gaspard? Gaspard who always got what he wanted.

Everything except her. Perhaps that was part of why he wanted her.

Before she left, she'd begun to fear what he might do, to her even, to make her marry him. The thought made her shiver and clench her fist. More of the fire's crimson filled her bones, and she stoked it to combat the gray.

Six weeks. A different village each day. Beast could have explained that *before* she'd entered the castle.

But if that much of her dreams was true, how much else was?

"It's a vegetable soup." Beast said it as if she were a complaining child refusing to eat.

Belinda glanced questioningly from her nearly full bowl to Beast, but he was studiously avoiding her gaze.

Had he actually, really looked at her even once since entering? A bit more red heated her bones.

"In case you're wondering, Miss Lambton," he continued, "I did *not* eat both the deer and the bear. I arranged for them to be dressed and left at the house of the local clergyman. He will know who has need of the meat. I had no desire for it."

Belinda's spoon clanked to her bowl, splashing broth across the tablecloth. "I didn't think that!"

"You must be very dense not to, or very naïve," he snapped, pain giving his voice a cutting edge.

Belinda's jaw worked several times before words could coalesce into solid thought. Not until she threw her napkin down beside her bowl was she able to throw out a reply. "I may be a fool in some ways," she spat, "but not in the way you suppose. I can tell a dangerous person from an angry, embarrassed, self-pitying one!"

He'd nearly died for her.

But he could still be a jerk.

Belinda glared at Beast, whose hairy face was showing signs of shock. *Not used to being told unpleasant truths, are you?* She considered storming out of the room, but since she could only walk one foot a minute, she didn't think it would be the dramatic exit her anger warranted. Nor very mature of her. *Beast* might run away from trouble and responsibility, but Belinda would hold her ground.

Starting now anyway.

Beast cleared his throat and looked away. "It's comforting to know there are brains behind your beauty."

The sarcasm of his tone wasn't lost in its deep rumbling, but Belinda didn't honor it with a response.

Both she and Beast turned their attention to the meal and didn't speak again until the servants came to clear away the food.

Though too angry to give him a full inspection, Belinda suspected Lyndon, wisely silent across the table, was trying not to smile.

৩৯৩

BELINDA'S ANGER, like her energy, waned by the end of dinner, as her pain and exhaustion waxed. Through Lyndon's kind insistence, and his arm for support, she found herself joining him and Beast in the library instead of slipping away to her room.

"Do you enjoy dramatic readings, Miss Lambton?" Beast asked politely as they entered the bright, warm library. Lyndon left her at the door and went to arrange chairs by the fire.

The blood fled Belinda's face. "Um ... ah ... I don't have much experience with them." Not good experience anyway. Those with difficulty reading didn't like such games, which were often played at their expense.

"A neglect we should remedy." Beast plucked a book from a library shelf, his back to her.

Feeling Lyndon's intent gaze, and fearing her face gave away too much, Belinda turned away and sought her little desk in its quiet nook.

"There's a comfortable chair by the fire for each of us, Miss Lambton." Beast gave her a curious glance as he made his way to his enormous wingback chair.

She opened her mouth to claim she was tired and needed to return to her room, but found she couldn't. *You've a reading spell now. Stop cowering.*

But would her tongue, unaccustomed to the swift passage of her eyes over words, be able to follow? Swallowing back painful memories, Belinda joined Beast and Lyndon by the fire, uncomfortable in a comfortable chair. *You'd prefer Beast propose in whatever respectably sneaky way he has planned rather than be forced to creep into your room and ask you while you're sleeping, wouldn't you?* she reminded herself.

"Take your time to read over it." Beast passed her a gold-embossed copy of *Jane Eyre*. She clutched the book with sudden gratitude—not only did she love the story but was familiar with it from her father reading it to her.

"Perhaps Miss Lambton does not care for reading aloud," Lyndon said as he took a tray of tea and cocoa from the air.

"I've never known Miss Lambton to be at a loss for words," Beast said with an amused gleam in his eyes as he gave her a sideways glance, "so I doubt reading aloud would be an unpleasant experience for her. But if she does not wish to read with us, she may merely sit and enjoy. If I do say so myself, Lyndon and I are superior performers."

Piqued, Belinda leaned back in the wide, well-cushioned mate to Beast's giant wingback and forcibly dispersed all signs of nervousness. "In that case, I shall have to join you, if only to allow you, by having a comparison, to be *superior*."

"As I said, she is never at a loss for words, however incongruent they might be with my meaning." Accepting a sturdy mug of tea from Lyndon, Beast eased into his chair. "Will you begin, Miss Lambton, when you are ready, with the first passage marked by a ribbon?"

Belinda opened the volume to the indicated passage, and after a moment's perusal, read aloud of poor Jane's terror in the red room. Too piqued to be more than mildly nervous, she did a passing fair job, infusing as much passion and horror into her untrained voice as she could, and trying to repress her joy at being able to read so well aloud. As Lyndon read superbly of Mr. Rochester in his guise as the old fortune teller, Belinda conceded that Beast's boast of Lyndon was not a faulty one.

As Lyndon finished, Beast took up the volume with an air of confidence Belinda envied. And made note of: Beast, in his former life as a man, had been trained in performance or speaking, or both.

His voice was rich and deep, and whether it was his voice or the effect of a warm fire, hot cocoa, and having at last found a position that did not aggravate her injuries, sleep made a determined fight for Belinda and was near to winning. She just noticed between blinks that Beast looked often between her and Lyndon, like a well-trained speaker making eye contact. Her lips twitched and waited for the particular passage where Beast would make certain to, very briefly, make eye contact with her alone.

"And your will shall decide your destiny," he proclaimed, a hint of tightness to his voice. His gaze, warily, met hers. "I offer you my heart, my hand, and a share of all my possessions."

Forcing herself to momentary alertness, Belinda caught his eye, fluttered her eyelashes, smiled sweetly in return, and opened her mouth.

"You play at a farce," he continued hastily, his falsetto voice for Jane even higher than before, "which I merely laugh at."

Oh, I never joke about such things. Belinda let her head rest in the cushioned corner between the chair wing and the back, content now to listen. Sleep renewed its attack on her and was only kept at bay by a reluctant acknowledgement of the rudeness of falling asleep during Beast's excellent performance.

At last, the great chestnut tree was struck by lightning, a fitting omen to Mr. Rochester's proposal, and Beast put away the book.

"Poor Jane," Belinda said sleepily as Beast took up his tea again. "And poor Mr. Rochester. He should have known his secret would come out in time. They always do."

"His secret should have come out," Beast said, lowering his teacup to gaze at her, a strange intentness to his expression, "for he was doing wrong and was wronging another. But must secrets always come out? Has a man no right to keep any?"

Or a beast no right? "Does a secret never wrong another?" said Belinda, snuggling a little deeper into the corner of the cushioned chair, her eyes drifting shut.

"It will always affect another, but whether another is wronged depends on the secret. But let us consider the right of the secret bearer. If the secret is his alone, surely he has as much right to guard it as a man does his corporeal property."

Not meaning an answer by it, Belinda huffed. Beast must really want to keep his anonymity. As if Lady Violetta would let her figure it out anyway.

Beast took the huff as a challenge. "Are not a man's thoughts, his plans, hopes and dreams, even his name, his own to hold?" he pressed.

Belinda's lips curved in a lazy smile of confirmation.

"Just as much as a lady's location?" He countered that smile.

One eye cracked open to tell Beast exactly what she thought of that underhanded blow. But her eyelid soon drifted down again, and whether the message had been properly delivered or not, Belinda found she didn't really care. A warm fire, lingering pain, and deep, soft voices had too great a somnolent effect. "I concede," she said softly.

There was a heavy pause, as if Beast had words ready he suddenly didn't know what to do with.

Belinda's breathing had just reached the rhythm fit for sinking beneath the crest of consciousness into the realm of sleep, when Beast's voice, an unwanted preserver of consciousness, buoyed her.

"Surely you're not going to sleep there?"

"It's comfortable," she managed, with more of an effort to *not* wake fully than otherwise. "You said so yourself."

"I said *my* chair was comfortable."

"This is its mate."

"But it's still not mine."

"Did you steal it?"

"Miss Lambton ..."

"Why do you care so where I sleep? I'm not moving." Her lips curling automatically at Lyndon's chuckle, she ignored Beast's sighing mutter about a crick in the neck and her having enough injuries as it was. He lapsed into silence, and her breathing readied for a dive.

"Fine," Beast said at last. "*I'll* move you."

But Belinda didn't hear him.

THE NEXT DAY was much the same as the last. Pain and gray chill and sleep during the day, broken with bits of light from her dream of Beast and visits from Lyndon.

"Are you in pain, Miss Lambton?"

It took several blinks for Belinda to recognize the change in scenery from the misty castle gate to her bedroom, from Beast's hunted look to Lyndon's paternal expression of concern.

"Um ... not too much if I don't move," she answered sleepily, pushing herself up against her pillows. An open book toppled from her lap as she did.

"Are you awake enough to tell?"

"Yes." She grimaced as she propped herself up against her pillows. Settled, she smiled up at him, and his narrowed eyes relaxed. "Why? Was I crying out in my sleep?" Did she say aloud the things she was thinking about Beast and that horrible woman?

Lyndon picked up the book and straightened a folded page. He rubbed his thumb thoughtfully along the book's brown leather spine before answering. "Your expression was fretful, almost angry at times." He cocked his head to look at her fully, as if expecting a full answer. Why did Belinda not want to give it?

Despite the uncomfortable twisting of her stomach and the flush of her cheeks, or because of them, Belinda smiled brightly. "I'm not angry at you or Beast. You needn't worry."

Lyndon's face fell expressionless, but he wore the same air Belinda felt she had: that of one whose attention was entirely focused on sound. Footsteps, heavy but athletic despite that, passed quickly along the hallway. The door to Beast's room opened.

Lyndon glanced at the clock on the mantle, then turned his attention back to her. "Was it pain or a nightmare, Miss Lambton?"

Belinda started at his tone, serious and almost cold, and so much nearer than the hallway she'd been focused on. "Neither. More of a ..." What exactly was it? After learning about the rotating villages, "dream" seemed too close to a lie for her to be comfortable with. "Vision" was possibly too close to the truth. "Something like a strange dream." She added hurriedly, "Have you been here long? I do hope I wasn't snoring."

He regarded her a moment, then leaned back in his chair. "As to the first, yes. I thought I would join you while Beast was occupied. You were asleep, and so obviously dreaming, I stayed to make sure you weren't lapsing into a fever or in need of someone to wake you from a nightmare."

"That was kind of you."

"You have a curious sleep schedule, Miss Lambton. I looked in on you yesterday while Beast was occupied, and you were sleeping then."

A ridiculous, guilty flush blazed across Belinda's cheeks. "I've noticed insomnia is not a problem in this castle."

He arched an eyebrow, and Belinda's hand fisted around her comforter. What if she did dream of Beast? She didn't ask for them, and they affected no one—by rights, by Beast's own admission, it was her secret to keep.

Lyndon's gaze swept from her face to her hand, contemplatively, and he relaxed in his chair. "Would you like to play a game of chess?"

An hour later, Lyndon took his leave. He paused at the door, a serious expression falling over him again as he turned to her. "As to your fear of snoring, you do not snore ... but you do talk. Miss Lambton, I am to return to Beast's family in a few days. If there is anything regarding my master's safety you know, you must tell me. Please tell me."

Belinda nodded and lowered her gaze, and he left. Her thoughts drifted back to her dream.

The lady called to Beast. She'd almost stopped doing that, as if finally realizing that wouldn't halt him. Yet today's calls were clear, guiding in reverse. Her cry came from the left. Beast darted right. Further along his path, two burly men crouched in the rhododendrons.

"Look out! She's herding you. Use your nose like a proper beast!" Belinda had thought. Like the lady, Beast had been growing wiser too, more scent, more sound to aid in his role of fox in the morning chase. "Careful, Beast!"

Beast sniffed the air, doubled back, and sheltered among the cedar boughs until the woman passed and left with the men.

Sighing, Belinda collapsed against her pillows. *If* her dreams were real, then she had nothing to tell Lyndon Beast couldn't tell him himself.

Speaking of *tell*, the next time she saw that enchantress, she'd have a thing or two to say about her hijacking Belinda's dreams without her consent. And heaven forbid Beast know she was dreaming about him. He might be a beast, but she had little doubt he'd lost his masculine ego.

Lunch was served shortly, which did a great deal toward disentangling the twists of defensiveness and confusion in her chest that Lyndon's questions had evoked.

Only after lunch was put away did she realize Lyndon had left her a book: the copy of *Jane Eyre*. A passage toward the end was marked for her: *"It is time some one undertook to rehumanize you," I said, parting his thick and long uncut locks; "for I see you are being metamorphosed into a lion, or something of that sort. You have a faux air of Nebuchadnezzar in the fields about you, that is certain: your hair reminds me of eagles' feathers; whether your nails are grown like bird's claws or not, I have not yet noticed."*

Belinda huffed a laugh as she read it. If Lyndon had hopes of her undoing Beast's metamorphosis, he would be sadly disappointed. As would the enchantress. There was more than one way to skin a beast down to its human hide, but she didn't know any of them.

And yet ...

She was not a woman to give in to gray.

Belinda tapped the book to her chin. She'd inadvertently roused the protector in Beast once before. Perhaps she could do it again—in a manner less uncomfortable to herself—and in doing so, clear away some of those eagles' feathers from other areas as well.

AT DINNER, they talked of the weather, which Belinda discovered to be a more stirring topic than she anticipated. A storm was brewing and was sure to burst upon them in the next few days. To her further surprise, she ascertained that Beast found the flash of deadly bolts of electricity and the deafening cracks of thunder exciting. She wasn't quite sure if that had anything to do with a change of heart, but she stored the information away as a possible sign of courage for non-life-threatening events and proof of his not total lack of interest in activities more exciting than turning pages. Out of curiosity, she let slip, with a slight exaggeration, her own dislike of storms. Beast perked up ever so slightly, and a contemplative light crept into his eyes. Belinda smiled to herself.

After dinner, when Beast pulled from some hidden location a copy of *Much Ado About Nothing*, she was very nearly affronted. Did he think she would abscond with every book containing a proposal?

It wasn't a bad idea actually.

But she couldn't find a pillowcase that large.

So she chose to take the high road instead. "I'll take the part of the fair Beatrice, shall I?" she said before Beast could give his usual commands in that regard. "Lyndon, you should be Benedick. You have just the right voice for the part."

"I'm pleased you think so, Miss Lambton," Lyndon said with admirable nonchalance. "His is a most entertaining role."

Beast merely passed them each a worn copy of the play and said firmly and without concern, "Benedick's part is mine. You may have Claudio, Lyndon. Miss Lambton will also read for Hero."

Despite losing the privilege of frustrating Beast, Belinda found herself enjoying the reading and was surprised as Lyndon and Beast paused in their reading to indulge in laughter, playing both characters and themselves as audience.

Belinda joined in their merriment, nearly forgetting the play's purpose until its end. That dialogue was for Benedick and Beatrice alone, and Beast had proven he could play the part with all the delightful spirit Benedick deserved. She would give Beatrice equal life. For once, Belinda thought as she remembered the mortification of Gaspard's declarations of intending to marry her, she could enjoy a proposal.

"Soft and fair, friar," Beast said, leaning forward in his seat and looking at her. "Which is Beatrice?"

Belinda straightened her shoulders proudly and flourished her hand before her face, mimicking the removal of a mask. "I answer to that name. What is your will?"

"Do you not love me?"

She cocked her head and raised her chin, as if she could look down on the towering Beast. "Why no; no more than reason."

Beast's teeth showed in a slight, ghastly smile before he banished it. "Why, then our uncle and the prince and Claudio have been deceived: they swore you did."

"Do you not love me?"

"Troth, no; no more than reason."

"Why, then my cousin Margaret and Ursula are much deceived; for they did swear you did."

"They swore that you were almost sick for me."

"They swore that you were well-nigh dead for me."

"'Tis no such matter. Then you do not love me?"

"No, truly, but in friendly recompense."

"Come, cousin," Lyndon said, a surprising interruption to their banter, "I am sure you love the gentleman." Changing voices, he added, "And I'll be sworn upon't that he loves her; for here's a paper written in his hand." Leaning forward, he pulled a folded square of paper from his pocket and handed it to Belinda, who dutifully read it, her brow creasing as she did, for it was Beast's next line. "A halting sonnet of his own pure brain, fashion'd to Beatrice," Lyndon continued, then shifted to a third tone, "And here's another writ in my cousin's hand, stolen from her pocket, containing her affection unto Benedick."

"A miracle! Here's our own hands against our hearts," Beast said, one hand nearly swallowing up a steaming cup on a newly placed tray beside them. The aroma of warm chocolate called to Belinda, but she wouldn't let it distract her. Glancing between her and the cup, Beast continued with the most important line of the night, to his mind anyway, Belinda thought.

Beast settled his blue eyes on her, his manner entirely too confident for Lady Violetta to be pleased. "Come," he said, "I will have thee: but, by this light, I take thee for pity."

Belinda checked a smirk. *Pity? What a blow to her vanity! And here's to yours, Beast.* "I would not deny you; but, by this good day, I yield upon great persuasion; and partly to save your life, for I was told you were in consumption."

"Peace! I will stop your mouth." Beast rose from his chair, reached hers in two steps, and hunched over her, coming close enough for Belinda to smell the lavender scent of his clothes. Her heart stuttered as the stage direction glared up at her: *Kissing her.*

"Why, Beast!" Her affected cry of mock indignation cracked as she pressed back in her chair. "Don't you dare act that ou—"

With a very un-beast-like twinkle in his eyes, he shoved a cup of hot chocolate in her hand and returned to his seat, not even missing his next lines.

Belinda melted against the chair back, held her cup to her mouth, and tried to pretend her cheeks were heated only from the aromatic steam. *Thank goodness for the curse.* Those eyes in a human face would be dangerous to a woman's heart. Not that Belinda was prone to romantic foolishness.

They all slipped into silence as the play concluded, watching the fire and savoring their drinks. She, wanting to confirm a suspicion and still genuinely pained and exhausted, allowed herself to bob along the waves at the boundary of sleep and wakefulness.

And so she made no protest when Beast quietly chided her for falling asleep in her chair and then carried her gently upstairs and gave her to the maids to ready her for bed.

Beast has a protector's heart. Belinda mused over the discovery as she settled into her covers. Lyndon told her to ascertain what virtues Beast possessed, if he had any that could be kindled to break the curse. Now she knew of two: a protector's heart and generosity as a host. Perhaps even a sense of humor, she added, remembering his laughter and twinkling eyes.

Unlike his smile, Belinda decided as she fell asleep, Beast's laughter was not ghastly, merely deep and rumbly and warm.

CHAPTER 8

A miracle! *Here's our own _hands_ against our hearts.* Belinda tossed Lyndon's note from the reading into the fire. He'd left *it* a second time when he visited her the previous morning, along with a cryptic comment about a rose missing another petal. Was that a euphemism for Beast growing older?

And why that quote? Was he recommending she invade Beast's private correspondence to learn more of his heart? That was hardly an honorable thing to do. Belinda gave the note curling and blackening in the fireplace another glance, one of shock and suspicion. Did *Lyndon* read Beast's mail? He didn't seem the type.

Shaking her head, she straightened gingerly. It had now been several days since The Incident and the beginning of the nightly reading. Her legs, side, and arm were much better, though far from normal. She stroked the powder blue satin of her gown. Was it possible to return to normal, after being pampered and sedentary so long? Would she even be able to run fast enough to escape Gaspard by the time she returned home?

It was time to get active again, but she'd beaten the sun up. She couldn't go out. Clean her chambers? She looked around her spotless room and her chest tightened.

She'd dust the library. Surely that would keep her occupied for a time.

Taking her shawl against the morning's chill, she crept down to the library, not wanting to disturb anyone with her early morning perambulations to collect a cleaning cloth and get to the library. Her heart fell as she pushed open the ornately carved door: the normally cheerful room was as empty and lifeless as its cold hearth. As if she expected any different before the sun rose. She stifled the strange feeling that she had expected something else.

After seeing to the fire, Belinda began the exhausting task of hunting for dust. When that proved more stressful that not, she chose a book and marched resolutely to her little desk, which had been neglected of late. She did not, however, search for letters among the papers on the table adjacent to Beast's desk. If it did occur to her his name might be on them, she ignored the dishonorable thought and focused on her book. It would be an unprincipled act to read private mail. Her father would never approve of using such means to gain her own end even if that end aided him as well.

Some time later, the chamber maid entered to see to the fire, but noticing it was done, backed out. Belinda ignored her too.

Two chapters later, that unearthly sleepiness began to creep over her, *at last*. Another early morning venture.

And her about to crash onto a desk and possibly be drooling over a book when Beast found her.

Her vision half in the morning mist and half on the library furniture, Belinda stumbled across the carpet, guiding herself on chair backs and free-standing shelves until she collapsed into her chair by the fire.

The dream was much the same as the others, except that rain and a howling wind chased Beast back to the castle rather than the lady. And that Lyndon went ahead of Beast to the village and passed a letter off to a cloaked man. The man clapped Lyndon on the shoulder with easy familiarity and rode away. His athletic form was vaguely familiar.

It was the smell of coffee that woke Belinda.

She opened her eyes to see steam rising from a delightfully scented porcelain cup on the little table beside her chair. Across from her, Beast sat, practically a part of his chair, holding his mug in front of his face, as if it could hide his toothy smirk.

"I'd say you're up early, but you aren't actually up."

"I was. Briefly." *And if I'm not up, it's your fault.* Belinda sat up, quickly taking up the coffee cup as an excuse to look away from Beast's bright blue look of amusement. He picked up a book on the care of roses, and soon breakfast arrived for both of them.

There was quite a crowd for her normally solitary morning meal, Belinda thought grimly as a tray appeared before her: Herself. Beast. And the storm that had followed Beast to the castle.

Lightning flashed so sharply beyond the stained glass windows that even an enchantress would have had a difficult time competing for brilliance. Belinda's cup rattled onto its saucer and her shoulders scrunched as she counted, bracing for the peal of thunder.

And waited for the scorn that usually followed her flinching. But Beast wasn't her sisters. He ostensibly paid no more mind to her than to the thunder, and somehow, realizing that, she ate in greater peace than she expected.

After the breakfast trays had been taken away, Belinda let her restless feet guide her from the library for that tour of the castle she'd promised herself when she arrived. She gawked properly at the towering entryway, laughed to herself at the enchantress's clever or sometimes ridiculous transformations, and tried to imagine how the castle might look after the curse was broken.

Her tour took her up stairs and down corridors she'd had no reason to traverse before. She was not, understandably, to invade private apartments, but most of the rooms on the wing currently under investigation appeared to be guest chambers. All decorated with thorned vines and dead flowers. Lots of dead flowers. Was Lady Violetta trying to tell Beast something or had she run out of ideas? The flower of his youth was wasting away, perhaps?

Taking a narrow staircase at the end of the lengthy corridor, she followed its curves up into the tower of the castle. This particular tower, if she guessed her location properly, had a twisted appearance and numerous spikes. Like intertwined vines studded with thorns.

It was a very tall tower, and its stones did little to shield her from the vibrations caused by the thunder. No warmth of fires reached this far either, and little light ventured in to touch the stone steps, beyond those raucous flashes of storm light. She wasn't quite sure why she was practically walking up into the heart of the storm, other than a stubborn determination not to cower before it again that day. So she kept going.

When the small windows revealed naught but darkening clouds, the stairway ceased, flattening out into a small antechamber of rough rock lacking the polish of the floors below. That didn't surprise her. But the open door, with candlelight and voices drifting from it, did.

Belinda froze, considered the likelihood that Beast had an insane wife locked away up here, shook her head, then slowly approached the half-open door. When was the last time she'd heard an easy, natural conversation between friends? Or between an old married couple, as the sometimes tender, sometimes teasing tone of these two suggested? There was also another set of voices, sounding small and far away.

There was a break in the louder conversation, and Belinda started, realizing with a blush that she was leaning against the doorframe eavesdropping with a ridiculous smile on her face. She had definitely *not* been woolgathering about conversations between her future, silver-haired self and anyone else.

Did beasts turn gray with age? She rolled her eyes at the ridiculous question.

A sign above the lintel read "Observation Room," so she had no reason not to take the room at its word. "Hello?" she called as she stepped over the threshold.

Gasping, Belinda jerked back, grabbing the door with one hand and pressing the other to her chest. The rounded room stretched out from the castle wall, narrowing to a point some fifty feet beyond it. Rather like the inside of a very long thorn.

A glass one.

The room's walls, ceiling, and floor were transparent, providing excellent, and very disturbing, views of the swirling clouds and lightning bolts outside.

Belinda swallowed hard. *What? No spyglass to observe the neighbors? How disappointing.*

Not far into the room were two tables, a desk, and a few comfortable chairs. A tea kettle began to whistle happily on a wood-burning stove just beyond those. Crossing her eyes, Belinda could make out two servants, one rising from the desk chair and one standing beside the stove. That second set of voices stilled.

On the desk, visible through the male servant, was a silver hand mirror resting on a stand, the apparent focus of the otherwise barren room. Like many of the rooms below, the mirror had a pattern of thorned vines and flowers. Stylized roses, Belinda decided, and wondered. *A mirror in an enchanted castle*. This was an observation room, but of what and by what means? The mirror's reflection, though not plain to her where she stood, didn't seem the right blend of colors for the room around her. Or more to the point, the clouds around her.

"Oh, miss!" said the woman by the stove, worry in her tone. "Should she be up here?" she whispered to her husband.

"Should you?" the man asked Belinda.

Belinda shrugged. "I know of no particular reason why I *should* be here, nor any reason why I *shouldn't*. This is an observation room, and I am observing the castle. Only personal chambers were forbidden to me."

The man shrugged as well then, and Belinda fancied he swung his arm out toward the walls, away from the mirror. "Observe away then. Just don't faint."

A smile twisted Belinda's lips. Oh, he was a clever one. "I'll try not to." Belinda smirked to herself at the thought that an invisible man couldn't very well block the sight of a mirror, or make too much of a fuss if she sat on him. After all, it was a long flight of stairs, and she could use a rest. But after a stroll around the room, to throw them off guard.

The wife offered Belinda a cup of tea, which Belinda declined, suspecting there was only water enough in the pot for two cups. Hands behind her back, Belinda strolled casually along one length of the room, catching glimpses through the swirling clouds of forests and gardens below. Eventually, the room narrowed too much for her to stand.

Catching the wall for support during a tremor caused by a thunderclap, she shut her eyes in preparation against yet another blinding flash. She had a mere second's wait, then she opened her eyes and pointed her feet back toward the desk and door. There was really no point in dissembling her interest and remaining there longer than strictly necessary.

"Who are you watching in the enchanted mirror?" she asked, walking hastily, but with dignity, back to the occupied section of the thorn-room. It couldn't be Beast. Otherwise, Lyndon wouldn't be so interested in her dreams.

The man sighed softly and rose again from his chair at the desk and stepped aside. "Would my lady care to see for herself? A picture is worth a thousand words."

Unless a word—a name—is all that would be telling. Belinda perched on the edge of the chair and looked into the mirror's surface.

It was a room, richly furnished, and extravagantly lit with candles. It was an uncursed room. Decorated in kingdom colors and hung with a map of New Beaumont, a flag of New Beaumont, and portraits of famous kings and generals, it bore equal signs of wealth and love of New Beaumont. Near the rear of the room, a large man sat behind a large desk in an intimidating duo of largeness. The man's eyes were even the same chestnut brown as the desk and just as hard. Only, the desk lacked his haughty air. A trim man stood before him, showing him some figures on paper. Though the second man's clothes were not as fine, they gave an impression of a lower kind of authority. His look, at the moment, however, was cowed. The steward?

"Incredible!" she exclaimed. "I've never seen anything like it. Are the mirror's observations random or are they controlled?"

Beast's servant hesitated. "My master is concerned for his family."

That was Beast's father? Barely keeping the exclamation to herself, Belinda leaned forward to better observe the man, something in her gut revolting at the idea of a blood connection between her beast and that arrogant bully. Not that she could find a physical resemblance between the man and Beast in his current form. Switching her attention to the room again for clues, she studied a crest on the wall she'd missed earlier, before remembering the second set of voices. She reached for the mirror's handle, curious if the faraway voices would return if she touched it.

"Please, my lady."

Belinda caught the sense of movement, as if the man reached out his hand to her in a pleading motion to match the tone of his voice. Shame warmed her chest. Had Beast no privacy and his servants no right to try to maintain that?

What of the privacy of the subjects of the servant's observation?

Beast has his reasons.

Surely.

"Forgive me," she said quickly. Drawing back her hand, she stood. "Beast has many secrets, and I shall have to content myself with being surrounded by an air of mystery."

Wishing the couple a good day, she jogged down the tower steps, deciding to be less nosy and more musically inclined. There was nothing like a concerto to drown out the thunder.

Beast and Lyndon joined her in the music room, listening, praising, and accompanying her. She played while they sang. Lyndon played while she and Beast sang. Lyndon listened while she played the piano and Beast played a cursed version of a bass violin that looked rather like a tortured donkey but sounded superb. Beast was a ... person of many talents.

⚜

LONG AFTER MIDNIGHT, a sudden flash of light lit up Belinda's room, highlighting her reflection in the gilded, floor-length mirror across the chamber like a spectral vision.

Rather pretty, is she? She'd almost forgotten Lyndon's comment to Beast what seemed so long ago. Though her heart still pounded from the crack of thunder that swiftly followed the lightning, she couldn't stop a bittersweet smile. She was ghastly pale in the mirror's reflection, but Belinda knew she still had the silky hair, bright eyes, and striking figure that had caused her to lose the friendship of her jealous sisters and many likewise-envious village lasses. That had gained her the interest of many a man, some of whom had no right to be interested in any woman, let alone her.

How fortunate she was to be blessed with beauty.

Yet Beast had thought her pretty. He, whoever he was, must have lived in the best circles and seen many attractive women, all educated in the best finishing schools and pampered by numerous servants. All unlike Belinda with her simple clothes and self-styled hair. Yet he'd found her pretty enough to emphasize with a snarl that he wasn't interested. He didn't deny her beauty, but he also never made her uncomfortable about it.

Rolling from one side to the other, Belinda tried to squash the feminine vanity that thought brought, but she couldn't. What had Beast looked like before his curse? Would she think him handsome? Or too foppish to earn that designation, no matter how fine his features? Who was he really, a stump or a scrawny sprout?

And how could she use that knowledge to free him and help her father regain his former life and attain her own freedom from Gaspard? *That* was what she should concern herself with.

In the wee hours, the storm unabated, Belinda crept down to the library, feeling better with more stone between her and the storm and less air between her and the ground. And perhaps ...

The library fire was still bright and warm. Beast was asleep in his chair. A folded missive sat on the table beside him, only lacking a seal to be ready. Wrinkled, handwritten pages lay tossed about his feet.

Shaking her head, she bent to retrieve the discarded sheets. He was a messy thing, far too used to servants picking up after him.

Perhaps too unconcerned about unscrupulous servants—or guests—reading his correspondence as well. If Beast could spy on who-knew-whom, then perhaps she could—

The tip of the last crumpled sheet was tucked between her fingers when Beast shifted in his chair and said in a voice softer and more rumbly than usual, "Leave my messes to myself or the servants. Go to sleep, Miss Lambton. In your chair."

Startled, she glanced between Beast and her chair. A blanket of wool the color of sunlit sky warmed her place in it, as if waiting for her. Her fingers closed automatically around the pages, folded them neatly, and tucked them into the space between her seat's cushion and arm as she sat, marveling and grateful that Beast was letting her stay. Belinda snuggled between the soft cushions of the chair and the warm blanket, closed her eyes, and listened to Beast's even breaths.

Despite the cracks of thunder that shook the window panes, causing even the castle stones to tremble in reverence, Belinda slept.

CHAPTER 9

Belinda had something in her hand when she woke the next morning, stiff, bleary-eyed, and still tired. Between blinks and squints, she ascertained that it was a rumpled letter. Had Beast left her a message? He was no longer in his chair.

As she smoothed the parchment between her fingers, her brain slowly woke and reminded her of the previous day's events. She re-folded the half-opened letter and stuffed it back in its pocket between the cushion and the chair arm.

Despite Lyndon's hint, Belinda Lambton was not stooping to spying on Beast.

By letter, anyway. She couldn't help her dreams.

Belinda hurried upstairs, determined not to still be in her dressing gown when her dreams caught up with her. A maid was just finishing up her hair when Belinda's hairbrush yanked her attention to itself. She'd been brushing her hair when Lady Violetta first visited, the enchantress who made her dream. Her dreaming about Beast's jaunts proved she was *meant* to be spying on him, didn't it? For whatever reason, Lady Violetta didn't wish her to know exactly who Beast was

—or wasn't supposed to tell her—but there was no reason Belinda couldn't do as much spying as her itchy nose allowed. To aid The Uncurse Plan, of course. Besides, Beast's parents wanted him uncursed, and the letters were likely written to them.

As soon as the maid released her, Belinda marched downstairs and retrieved the letter from her chair. She arranged it according to the scratchy numbers handwritten on the bottom of each of the three sheets, each written nearly full on both sides, and read. Her cheeks grew red as she did. The letter was addressed to his parents, as she supposed. There were a few paragraphs concerning her, but she didn't have the courage to read those. What attracted her attention—and more than a trifle of her fury—was a lengthy discussion of the naval maneuvers of New Beaumont and New Grimmland—which he'd refused to speak to her about—and other matters of state before comments on what she assumed were family matters. Why had he pretended indifference concerning those to her?

Tossing the letter on the little table beside her chair, she grabbed the neatly folded, unsealed letter on the table beside Beast's chair, all compunction lost to other sensations. The red of her face deepened as she skimmed this single sheet.

Lips pressed together, she retrieved the thick, rumpled letter and stared between it and the pristine, thin one. In her left hand were six sides of paper with a well-reasoned and articulated discussion of family and state matters written in a manner that suggested an interest far greater than mere polite responses to questions asked. In her right, one side of flippant, borderline disrespectful nothings.

It was all she could do not to crush that single sheet. *Why, that deceitful, conniving, underhanded coward of a Beast!* He didn't need a change of heart—he cared about his family and the kingdom. And he was willing to study and learn for them—he cared enough to study in secret when he thought she wasn't watching in order to prepare responses to his parents' inquiries. He cared. He simply refused to admit it while playing the part of an indolent creature. But why? Why pour out his heart and mind on paper but not send it? He was hiding from something in that rug of a fur coat of his. Well, after she got ahold of him, he'd be hiding from h—

She blinked as a sudden tiredness washed over her.

After she dreamed, *then* she'd have a chat with Beast.

Her vision blurred as she felt her way to her chair and sat, resting her head against the cushioned wing. She wondered vaguely if that swish of the door signaled Lyndon's entrance to the library or hers to the dream.

The forest was quiet and Beast more anxious than usual. His nose continually sniffed the air, his neck swiveling side to side. Once, he listed to the right, a limp seemingly taking him by surprise. He walked onward a few feet, limping lightly, until shaking himself and glancing around the forest once more.

Belinda couldn't tell how long he paced within sight of the village, still and silent in slumber below him. The sun would soon rise brilliantly over the mountain peaks. No one would notice him then, and he knew it.

No one from the village, that is. Belinda looked around the dream, searching for the woman. Was she some plant of the enchantress's to torment Beast? Or someone else, someone he knew from before his curse?

No woman appeared, however, so Belinda studied the village in the growing light. It clung to a rocky mountainside, all somber stone buildings and walls, trees poking up here and there until gaining in density beyond the circle of homes and shops. The gray stone wept from the village, forming an orange-tinted ribbon of road in the sunrise, running over the mountainside to the pass leading to whatever lay beyond it.

There was something familiar about that sunflower-tinted gray-

ness. Belinda couldn't see far beyond Beast in the dreams, but she managed to shift her view just enough to read the sign on the larger village inn: The Dog and Barrel.

It was a village between her father's house and the capital. In little more than a week, her father would be staying there, as eager to return to her as she to him.

Beast's ears perked, his whole stance indicating alertness, and Belinda's attention hurried back to him. The woman approached from the village footpath. Beast sensed her and stole back toward the stream that marked the boundaries of his land.

The lady moved faster, the brush of her silk skirts loud enough to compete with the songs of morning coming from the forest canopy. Beast shifted into a jog. Belinda glanced back at the lady to gauge her progress. Her fingers tapped against a golden locket in time with her steps. She was smiling through her panting. Smugly.

Alarmed, Belinda jerked away to scout Beast's path. No men. So why that smug smile? She searched the paths Beast might take again and the woods around them. Small, furry creatures that shied from the bright light of day waddled through the underbrush, but no men.

There. Something off-white amid the leaves. A bit of a rogue's shirt?

No, a length of rope.

An accidentally unmasked length of rope tied between two trees.

Belinda surveyed again with a keener eye. All through the forest, camouflaged ropes were taut between trees, hidden and low. Beast was running toward one now.

Her vision sped: Beast running, tripping over a rope that snapped around his ankle; the woman standing over him, demanding Beast ask her what she knew he must; Beast, with defeat and horror in his face, asking. The scenes flashed again and again before her eyes, her heart pounding in the same impossibly fast pattern.

"Look out, Beast!" she cried.

Lyndon. She had to tell Lyndon. But the dream never gave her up before it was done.

But she talked in her sleep. And Lyndon intended to guard Beast through her dreams.

"Lyndon! Lyndon! There are tripwires hidden all over the forest."

That same forest began to shake.

"Tripwires! Lyndon, you must do something!"

It shook until Belinda felt her dream-self toppling. How was Beast still running? Why didn't it topple him before the ropes did?

"Belinda! Wake up!"

Her head bounced against the chair back as her body moved in something between a gentle nudging and a desperate shaking.

Blinking, Belinda caught Lyndon's arm. "I'm awake. He's on his way back, but she's littered the forest with tripwires. He can't smell those. You must go—"

Lyndon was already standing, pulling her up with him and dragging her out of the library to the front door. He pressed his pocket knife into her hand. "I can't interfere, but you can. Go!"

Belinda's legs caught the fast rhythm of her heart, and she darted past Lyndon as an invisible servant opened the door. Hiking up her skirts, she flew over the paved carriageway. A shiver ran up her spine as the forest beyond the castle wavered as she sped under the arched gate. Would it let her back in?

She crossed the stream and shot down the path Beast would be coming up. It ran parallel to the road, and she had no doubt the lady's thugs were waiting there for her call.

Belinda pumped her legs harder, her voluminous skirts nearly as loud in the forest as the lady's. Why did proposals always seem to involve burning lungs and running?

She leapt over a fallen tree and faltered in her landing, her scraped legs protesting as she fell. A squeak sounded low and to her left, sending her heart into a frenzied rhythm, one that wasn't helped by the sight of twin stripes of white on black disappearing into the bushes. Or by the scent barreling her way. *Oh no.* She scrambled back, gagging.

"Oh, Beastie." The saccharine call from ahead was smooth and self-satisfied.

Oh no, you don't. Belinda pushed up and ran. The smell clinging to her ran with her.

She might as well make use of it.

Ignoring the taut, tender skin of her legs, Belinda dredged up more sped and started flailing her arms. "Skunk! Rabid raccoon!" she yelled. "Skunk! Rabid raccoon!"

Light green fabric shifted among the trees ahead.

"Skuuuunk! Rabid raccoooon!"

Belinda tore past the wide-eyed lady, skidded to a halt, and raced back to her. A brownish furry leg was just visible in the bushes off the path. "Skunk! Rabid raccoon! Run, my lady!"

"What—!" she cried. Belinda grabbed her arm and pulled. The lady tumbled after her. "Unhand me—"

"Rabid raccoooon!" Belinda yelled over her and tugged her stumbling down the path, the lady alternately protesting and trying not to gag. "Come on! Before it gets you!" She added in a hop every few feet for effect and to avoid the occasional rope. "Racooooon!"

Twenty feet up the path, Belinda shoved the woman ahead of her. "Keep going! I'll see if it's following us." She sprinted back to Beast, darted past him, spun around twice and screamed, hopping with each cry, "There it is! There it is!" She ran ahead again, chunking the knife at Beast's foot as she leapt over the one loose rope end.

She met the woman coming back and spun her around, ignoring her protests, which were growing quite colorful verbally. They were also physically determined enough to make Belinda glad she'd once been used to hard labor.

"Thank goodness! We're saved!" Belinda pushed the lady past the last shrub and onto the dirt road, sending dirt shimmering onto their gowns and scaring away the remaining mist. A fine carriage and enough guards and footmen as proper for a high-born lady awaited.

"It's just bit a squirrel, and now they're both after us!" Belinda cried, dragging her to the carriage. "Quick!" she called to the mounted guards and servants lingering about the carriage. "There're dangerous wild animals coming. You must get away! Your mistress isn't safe."

The guards looked to one another and to their mistress before a footman jumped down to open the carriage door. One guard, a man with a regal, military bearing and scars on his face, dismounted and strode to Belinda and the lady. As he approached, Belinda realized he wasn't wearing a guard's uniform but a soldier's of rank.

Belinda's steps faltered as her eyes met his. They were a familiar blue. But surely *his* eyes were his own and no one else could have them.

The lady slipped from Belinda's grasp. "You fool! You've ruined everything!" Her hand clashed sharply against Belinda's cheek.

Belinda fell back, blinking away tears as her hand covered her stinging cheek. She deserved that, but *ouch*. She was too shocked to notice the fire still burning in the woman's chestnut-colored eyes and the well-manicured hand pulling back for another strike until the blue-eyed man grabbed the woman's wrist.

"Leave her be, Lucrezia." He said it with a calm authority. She'd heard that voice before: he was the hero and bandit chaser.

"I *found* him, Robert," the woman hissed, jabbing her free hand threateningly at Belinda. "And *her* stunt let him get away. All these months, wasted!"

Belinda backed quietly away toward the tree line.

"If he 'got away' then it's probably for the best," Robert said, with a quick glance at Belinda. She stilled.

Lucrezia quit struggling against his hold, though her thin lips and flaring nostrils didn't indicate a surrender. "Robert," she said, her voice turning sickeningly sweet, "you want me to talk to him, don't you? You know my way is best."

Robert opened his mouth, his eyes already expressing his disagreement, but no words came out. He raised his shoulder to brush at his ear.

"Robert," she said sharply, then her voice softened. "Listen to me, Robert. You know it's best. Now let me go."

Robert did, his eyes glazing. He tugged his ear.

Belinda's nose itched as she focused on that tugging of his earlobe.

"Stop touching your ear," Lucrezia said sharply as she stepped away from him. Belinda darted back to the safety of the line of bushes. Lucrezia ignored her and ordered Robert to hand her into the carriage. She turned back long enough to find Belinda. "Don't ever let me see you again," she hissed as she rapped on the carriage ceiling for the driver to go.

As the carriage rumbled away, Belinda let out a sigh and stepped back onto the road, finally regaining enough sense to try for a look at the carriage's markings.

"Make sure she gets a bath!" Belinda yelled after it. She winced and gingerly touched her jaw. It was only a hair from being out of joint. What an arm for a noblewoman.

"Thank you."

Barely stifling a scream, Belinda spun around.

Robert stood by his horse, watching her.

"For what?" she croaked, lowering her hands.

He gave her a sad smile. "Do you need any assistance with the *dangerous wild animals*? Or a ride home?"

She took a step back, her gaze darting to the forest. She didn't like the way he'd said that. Irrationally disliked, given his kindness. But still ... "No, thank you, my lord." Her nose itched again as she met his gaze and studied his blue eyes. It wasn't just his eyes that were familiar. His entire face and build were. Had she seen him before, out of her dreams? Or a portrait of him? It was all she could do not to scratch her nose. "It's kind of you to offer."

As she studied him, he studied her. Unconsciously, Belinda straightened her dress and smoothed her hair.

"What's your name, my lady?"

My lady? Her? *Oh.* Striving for an air worthy of the elegant dress she wore, Belinda curtsied. "Miss Belinda Lambton, my lord."

"Do you live in the village there?"

"I can easily get home. You've no need to worry."

He quirked an eyebrow, but something in his expression suggested a confirmed suspicion. He bowed. "May I—" He glanced at the forest, indecision lingering in his gaze before his head bowed in defeat or hopelessness. "Are you certain I can be of no assistance?"

"No more than you have already. My jaw is ever in your debt."

A corner of his mouth curved, setting off the three thin, white scars on his cheek. Belinda's heart did a strange flip-flop. He nodded and mounted his horse. "It was a pleasure to meet you, Miss Lambton. I hope I shall see you again." He clicked to his horse and trotted up the road, opposite the carriage's path.

Not waiting for him to vanish beyond her sight, Belinda jogged back through the forest until reaching a set of trees with rope burns. The bushes shivered and shuffled at her approach.

"Beast, it's me."

Beast's head and shoulders appeared above a holly sapling,

his reply lost to Belinda as the excitement waned and her lungs' messages grew too loud to ignore.

She plopped down in the leaves next to Beast and doubled over, breathing heavily and laughing softly to herself.

Beast shifted to make room for her, his legs scooting out of sight further under the holly. "Are you insane?" He gaped at her, uncertainty, concern, and stupefaction blending in his expression.

That only made Belinda laugh louder. She leaned back on her hands, letting the laughter out and her breath catch up to her before she answered. Sobering, she sat up and took the knife from Beast, whose paws clearly weren't capable of using it properly. "Only when it's useful." She grinned at him. "Since I met you, it's come in handy more than once. King David would be proud. *He* only escaped the king of Gath."

Beast stared at her, his brows a bushy crown. Then he shook himself, that ghastly smile pulling back his lips from his teeth. "You're a marvel, Belinda Lambton."

"That's one way to describe me," she said, a touch of sarcasm in her tone.

"Truly, Belinda, I mean it."

Her knife stilled, and she met his gaze, searching.

"Truly," he repeated.

Belinda looked down at her knife, remembering many a less flattering description of herself. "Let's get you free, shall we? Can you pull your legs out from the holly?"

Beast obligingly drew them up, bending his knees and quickly clasping his ankles, covering them almost entirely. "The rope between the trees detached and wrapped my ankles together. A third connection chained me to that tree." He nodded to the mother holly beyond the sapling. "Just cut the rope to the tree and the one between my ankles for now. Lyndon will take care of the rest at the castle.

"What are you doing out here?" he continued. "I would've known if you'd followed me from the castle this morning."

"I dreamed about what was happening. And don't ask me how. I certainly didn't ask to have my sleeping habits tied to your daily constitutionals."

Beast gaped at her. Again. "You *dream* about me?"

"*Have visions* is more accurate. So don't flatter yourself too much." Belinda clicked the knife shut and rose to her knees. "And why is it so surprising? You have an enchanted castle and invisible servants. Can you stand?"

Wincing, Beast pulled his feet underneath him and allowed Belinda to help him up. He protested mildly when Belinda draped his arm over her shoulders but seemed sensible enough to know a determined woman when he met one. They started walking slowly, cautiously, up the trail.

"There's not really a rabid raccoon out here somewhere, is there?" he asked some minutes later, breathing heavily from his mouth and looking around warily.

"Not that I know of."

"But—"

She scrunched her nose against an odor she'd been *trying* to forget. "*But* there is an irritated skunk."

"I thought as much."

"Yes ... that was an unfortunate accident."

"But you made the most of it, and I'm grateful."

Belinda's cheeks pinked, but her eyes twinkled. "That lady was so busy trying not to gag she couldn't stop me from shuffling her off to the carriage. You should've seen the looks her servants were giving us, all wrinkled noses and wide eyes."

A deep chuckle rumbled in Beast's chest, and it warmed Belinda to hear it.

Then it died.

"Stay away from her, Belinda."

"She's hardly the sort of woman I'd choose for company."

"I meant ... stay away from me on these ... excursions. If she knew you were associated with me ... well, she's dangerous."

"That frilled peacock?" Belinda huffed. "*I'm* dangerous too."

Beast's laughter ended in a wince as a pronounced limp to his right leg unsteadied them. "Not in the same way."

Belinda stopped, insisting more than merely allowing Beast to lean on her to rest his ankle. She cocked her head to look up at him. "In what way is she dangerous?"

Beast eyed Belinda's cheek with an icy anger.

"Other than her being a fierce slapper?" Belinda asked, wondering why it was so unsettling to have Beast angry on her behalf.

"It's not something I can explain," he said, "but believe me when I say she's not to be crossed." He settled his foot down, easing his weight off Belinda, and they started walking again. "And your daily doses won't help against her."

"You know I don't take those, right?"

"I wasn't quite sure, to be honest, but I'm glad you don't." He paused a moment. "You know I don't fatten people up to eat them, right?"

"Well, I was a bit worried ..."

He looked down at her nestled against him, one hand around his back and his arm over her shoulders. Amusement lit his eyes. "Yes, I see how frightened you are of me." The spark of humor softened into one of curiosity and awe.

Belinda turned away, a warmth in her chest she didn't know what to do with. "About that day when you were hunting, I'm ... I'm sorry about what you had to do. But I'm grateful."

He stiffened and watched the path ahead. "It was the right thing to do, so I did it. ... And Belinda"—his tone pulled her eyes back to his—"it was worth it. Even without what you did today, it was worth it."

His expression warmed her and made her uncomfortable at the same time. "Thank you," she said quietly, looking away again quickly. Her gaze settled on the presumed safety of the path. Only Beast's feet got in the way of her view as he stepped forward. Blood was oozing down them to leave a crimson trail.

"Your ankles are bleeding an awful lot. Did you try gnawing the rope off?"

"So you do take me for a wild creature? And here I thought you'd decided I was civilized." Despite Beast's rumbling laughter, Belinda led them to a sizable boulder at the stream's edge.

"Let's rest a moment before we tackle that stream bank," she said. "It was a climb getting up that mountain."

Beast made no protest when Belinda dropped him on the boulder, but did when she knelt at his feet.

"Miss Lambton, take your rest. My ankles can wait until the castle." He scooted his feet away from her, but she merely followed them.

"A rope shouldn't cause this much bleeding. I can bind each ankle with strips of my petticoat. No sense getting blood on the castle floors again." She carefully lifted the fur trousers he wore over his cloth ones.

"Belinda, please—" He sighed, his shoulders slumping as she sucked in a breath.

"Your ankles are shredded!"

"Miss Lambton—"

Ignoring him, Belinda ran her fingers over the remaining rope. Her fingers stilled, and she gaped up at him, horror and anger in her eyes. "There are *rocks* and *glass* buried in the rope."

"It's an effective method of keeping one from slipping a rope."

"It's barbaric!"

"I told you she was dangerous," he said softly.

"Yes, but—" Belinda opened and shut her mouth a few times, then bent angrily over his foot and began sawing at the rope with her knife.

"Leave it for now."

Blinking furiously, she shook her head.

Beast reached down and put a gentle paw on her shoulder. "Leave it, please. The rope will keep dirt from the trail out of what wounds it covers."

Her hands stilled, then Belinda nodded and clicked the knife shut. Beast pushed himself up and offered her his arm. When Belinda eyed him doubtfully, he bared his teeth in a grin. "I can hobble just fine under my own power—and I don't want to give Lyndon any more gray hairs by hobbling in on your shoulder."

Belinda took his arm, and they slowly crossed the streambed. As the gates came into view, Beast's limp grew more pronounced, the furrows of his brow evident despite his shaggy fur.

"Belinda," he said seriously. "I meant what I said about her. If you hadn't been wearing the dress you are—had she not thought you a woman of fortune and protection—she would've horsewhipped you, not merely slapped you."

Belinda set her jaw, despite the lingering sting. "I can take care of myself."

"I thought so too once," he said so softly Belinda didn't hear him as Lyndon called to them from just inside the gates.

CHAPTER 10

The household was aghast as they entered, aghast at Belinda's smell and Beast's ankles. They were shuffled off to their rooms and "seen to." It was only after three baths and much perfuming that Belinda was considered "seen to" and allowed her freedom.

The library was empty as Belinda made for her desk. She grabbed a sheet of stationery and sketched the coat of arms on Lucrezia's carriage. She'd be more likely to match images without her nose itching than directly searching for the coat of arms in *Dirke's Peerage*.

She'd like to get her hands on that Lucrezia woman. Belinda had thought Gaspard bad, but this woman had crossed the line. And Belinda was not going to let her Beast marry anyone like that.

Belinda collected *Dirke's Peerage* and began her perusal. There were *a lot* of noble families in New Beaumont, she decided a half hour later, still searching.

The door opened, and she spun around guiltily yet didn't see anyone.

"Yes?" Belinda asked, searching for the telltale waver.

The rustle of a maid's dress as she curtsied preceded a quiet voice. "I beg your pardon, miss, but the master requested your presence for lunch in the conservatory."

"Me?" Belinda said, rising without realizing it. He'd never invited her to lunch before.

"Yes, miss," the maid said, a hint of amusement in her voice that steadied Belinda.

Of course he'd invite her. She *had* saved him, after all.

"Well, I am hungry, so you may tell him I'll join him presently."

Belinda was halfway to the conservatory when she realized she'd been distracted from her pursuit of identities, only without her nose itching. When she arrived and saw Lyndon's pursed lips and Beast's set jaw, she began to suspect her invitation was something of a distraction as well. One against Lyndon trying to convince Beast to give up his curse?

Why wouldn't Beast? What reason did he have to put up with the body of a beast and morning presentations and *that* lady?

That lady.

Belinda's footsteps stuttered as Lyndon guided her to a chair across from Beast, whose bandaged ankles were propped on a footstool. A gray chill settled in her chest.

❦

OBSERVATORIES WERE USUALLY INTENDED to be employed at night. Why would anyone question her for wanting to see the stars from a great height in the most unusual observatory there was?

Still, Belinda softened her steps as she spiraled her way up the tower sometime after midnight. When she reached the landing, she paused and listened. Hearing nothing and seeing no light, she tiptoed to the door of the observatory and lifted its latch.

Moonlight magnified through glass chased away the darkness. Dust motes drifting in the air shone like stars as Belinda stepped into the glass room. Her breathing suddenly eased, something about the stillness of the semi-dark and peaceful moonlight releasing a tightness she hadn't realized had constricted her heart. Forgetting about the ground far beneath her, she stared at the moon and its missing sliver, glorying in its light and the fine lines of its pockmarked face, before turning to the desk and its mirror.

Her chest tightened again as she set her candle beside the mirror and wrapped her fingers lightly around the mirror's silver handle. Its face was merely a reflection of hers.

She almost hoped it would stay that way, that it wouldn't answer her questions.

Belinda set her jaw and spoke, breaking the silence with a soft command. "Show me my father, please." Her breath puffed out visibly into the fireless room.

The image of a long lump under a thin sheet appeared, topped with a familiar head covered in loose gray hair resting on a pillow. Soft snoring faded out and back in as Belinda loosened and tightened her grip on the mirror's handle. Her fond smile was quickly strangled as her stomach tightened. The mirror answered familiar, possessive pronouns. She'd have to ask.

"Show me Beast's fiancée."

The mirror's face went blank.

Belinda slumped in her seat, a relief she wasn't willing to admit in her sigh. *Well done, Detective Lambton*, she told herself quickly, straightening. Beast wasn't retaining his curse as protection against an unwanted marriage. One theory down. Now she only had to make up more to cross off.

"Show me Beast's parents," she hurried on, not caring to

dwell on the lightness fluttering in her stomach, or the itch of her nose. An image of a violet appeared. "Yes, yes, I know. That's forbidden knowledge," she said, tapping her fingers on the desk.

"Show me Lucrezia, only child of the Duke of Marblue." Belinda had been able to "thoughtlessly" match the image of the coat of arms against *Dirke's Peerage* entries after lunch. Lucrezia was the daughter of the most powerful duke in the land, the king's loyal right hand man. Belinda didn't like what that meant about who Robert and Beast were.

A young woman appeared, asleep in a richly furnished room. It was *her* all right. It was a pity Belinda couldn't reach through the mirror and brain her, or at least slip her a sleeping potion so she'd not chase Beast tomorrow. He deserved at least one day of peace.

Well, not exactly. He could have it, if he wanted it enough.

But it was still a pity. It was also a pity Belinda couldn't use the mirror during the day without getting caught. She might catch Lucrezia plotting. Her lips settled into a mischievous tilt. Maybe Beast kept the curse to keep the mirror to be a spy.

"Show me Prince Rupert of New Beaumont."

The prince slept soundly, covers thrown back, windows open to the cool night air. He wore plaid pajamas. A faint red glow came from a hidden corner of the room. She snorted and rubbed her itching nose. *Plaid.* And not even in the kingdom's colors. She'd have to remember that should blackmail ever be needed, she said, distracting her thoughts.

The mirror at this time of night was less useful for spying than her dreams. She pulled her yellow shawl closer about her shoulders, letting the image of the sleeping prince fade away.

"Show me my father again, please." Smiling sadly, Belinda watched her father's chest rise and fall in a slow, peaceful rhythm. Moonlight gave a pale glow to the room as it flowed in through an open window. The prince might like it cold—which was understandable for him—but her father didn't. Was he still someplace so warm as that? He ought to be well on his way back.

If she gained him the reward Lady Violetta promised, would he be able to stay at home with her? Would they move? Or if travel was needed, Belinda could travel with him, free of Gaspard and independent of Beast. Once Beast transformed, she'd not be able to stay with him again. Or even speak with him.

After a few minutes, weariness and a touch of gray began to wear on her, and Belinda returned to her room. She fished her satchel out of the closet where she'd tossed it and pulled out Beast's discarded letter. Lyndon had gone to town that afternoon to hire a courier to send the disgraceful note-from-a-twitter-brained-fop. He was going to stay with them instead of returning to Beast's parents.

Sighing, Belinda sank onto her bed and slapped the stolen letter against her palm. She knew more now than she had before, but she was no further along in her quest to sever the curse and time was running out ... The time until the rose-metaphor-thing Lady Violetta mentioned happened, until her father returned, until Lucrezia caught Beast. The lady would stop at nothing to gain Beast's proposal.

Belinda's eyes narrowed as she touched a hand to her tender cheek. She'd stop at nothing to protect him.

And to earn the reward for her father, for she wasn't *that* devoted to Beast.

BELINDA WAS UP and outside the castle gates even before Beast. Even before the sun.

Her breath fogged, a lighter tone of silver than the misty

woods around her, as she puffed her way up the stream bank into the forest beyond. She had a moment's panic as her breath disappeared into the darkness. What if the castle didn't move until Beast stepped out the gate or beyond the stream? What if she were still at yesterday's village?

Calm down. Spells are midnight things. The castle's moved already.

Taking refuge behind a wide beech hugged by rhododendrons, she bounced up and down on her toes and rubbed her arms to stay warm and awake. She needed one, maybe two to three days at most, depending on the postal service, then Beast would be free of proposals and that lady. Until then ... A pistol-shaped lump in her bag banged against her leg. Some good old-fashioned scare techniques might work. Maybe.

Crunch.

Belinda crouched. The sound of leaves crushed underfoot in a familiar tread grew louder, slowed, then picked up again in a slightly different pattern before fading. Had he been sniffing the air when he slowed? Well, if he had, his nose failed him.

Crowing silently that she had escaped the dreaming by being out of the castle, she rose and backed out of the rhododendrons.

The dark green leaves suddenly blurred, and her heavy limbs dragged her to the forest floor. *Curses, curses, curses.* The dreams always were delayed, weren't they?

Beast slunk through the pre-dawn forest like an overgrown rabbit. Ripe for the picking by Huntress Lucrezia.

Something thumped. Like a body crashing onto something feeling closer to bedrock than a leafy mattress. Dropping to all fours, Beast spun around and raced to where Belinda lay sprawled out, half in the shrubbery.

"I thought I smelled something familiar." A heavy sigh from Beast ruffled her hair. "Meddling females," he groused as he carefully disen-

tangled her from the rhododendron and picked her up. His limp as he carried her out of the shrubbery caused her head to jostle against his chest. Why was he limping so? He claimed his ankles had healed.

He propped her sitting up against the beech trunk. "Serves you right. And, yes, I know you can hear me!"

Belinda slid down in a heap to the scaly beech roots as Beast began to limp away, quickly bringing him back again. "Remind me to start locking you in your room at night." Shaking his head, he straightened her out flat on her back, then took off his fur overcoat and stuffed it under her head.

"And don't drool on my coat. You'll mat the fur!" he called over his shoulder as he jogged off, his limp quickly disappearing into his normal easy, athletic gait.

But even that left him as the village neared and his caution grew.

Mat his fur indeed. Belinda's dream self crossed her arms. If he wanted to cower where he used to walk with such pride and ease, what was it to her?

Let the lady catch him. He deserved it.

Leaves crunched underfoot, and Beast stilled, then slipped into the shadows of a cedar. Belinda's heart thumped as she drew back and sought the source of the sound. But nothing claimed it.

No Huntress showed herself then, or at all that morning.

Taking a day off to plan another strike?

Sometime later, Beast returned to the castle, carrying Belinda in his arms.

Belinda woke in her chair in the library with a headache and a sense of lingering anxiety, and a bit of temper she couldn't put off any easier than the bits of leaves crushed into her hair.

CHAPTER 11

Belinda glared at Beast throughout breakfast, but he only smiled smugly. *Arrogant, overgrown teddy bear.*

"I'm going for a ride," she announced as the servants cleared the breakfast trays. "I'm taking my pistol, so there's no need for anyone to accompany me."

"There are no more bears on the estate, so go ahead. But do watch out for rabid raccoons."

With a huff, Belinda raised her chin and left.

She needed a new hat, she decided a quarter-hour later. But she couldn't very well ask for one that matched her gown when she was sneaking out, now could she?

Well, *sneaking* might be an exaggeration. They knew she was going out—she'd just dissembled about *where*.

She pulled the brown wool hat she'd worn to the castle nearly three weeks ago down to shade her face and guided her horse through the castle gates. She couldn't help a glance over her shoulder at the gates' twisted beams as she trotted beyond their short noontime shadows. Would she be able to return without Beast at her side?

She shook off the thought. Lady Violetta would make sure

she did. And if Beast had control of the barrier, then he ... probably would too.

Not that it mattered. Her work at the castle would be done after today.

Why did that make her heart feel like something the cat played with?

Using her memory of Beast's path in her dream to guide her, Belinda directed Marigold to the main road, then the village. She pulled the horse to a stop just outside it and dismounted. A lady of her supposed standing—if they ignored her hat and noticed only her dress and shawl—wouldn't be walking alone through town, much less riding alone. Walking was at least a little less conspicuous.

After rubbing Marigold's muzzle and promising to return soon, Belinda walked the rest of the way into the village with its wattle and daub houses and cobblestone streets. Her eyes searched for the post office, trying to ignore all else, including the stares and the guilty thumping of her heart. She *was* going to mail Beast's true letter to his parents, and when they saw it, they'd have to acknowledge a change of heart and have Lady Violetta remove the curse. The fool deserved the curse he clung to, but she was going to break it, so help her. If only to sleep in peace again, with no dreams. Belinda set her jaw, told off the heavy lump in her chest called a conscience, and marched on.

Thus, she entered town, head high, shoulders back, distracted.

And was promptly grabbed by the first hoodlum who saw her.

"Lindie pie!"

Belinda squeaked as a large pair of hands snagged her around the waist and spun her as if she were four years old.

"Put. Me. Down," Belinda snarled as she hit Gaspard on

the shoulder with all the strength of a lady with injured dignity.

The brute laughed but dropped her, catching her arm with a smirk as she struggled to get her footing. She tugged her arm away and glared at him as she straightened her hat.

"Sweetie pie, quit the act and give us a kiss. I've been worried about you. Where've you been?" Gaspard cupped his hands on her shoulders and leaned toward her. Giving her less distance to cover as she gave him a quick smack on the cheek —with her open hand.

Refusing to give him the satisfaction of seeing her shake her stinging hand, she stepped back and put her hands on her hips. "What are you doing here? And what did I tell you about calling me 'anything-pie'? It's *Miss Lambton*." Belinda scanned the village—which wasn't one near her own—for a post office or other likely spot to find a courier, or other excuse to get away.

Gaspard merely laughed, drawing her gaze briefly to his. The hint of anger and impatience in his eyes sent a chill down her spine. "I came on business."

"For the butcher shop?"

"For us, our future."

"I told you there is no 'us,' nor will there ever be."

"For big game then," he said, a familiar glow of pride and determination in his eyes.

By which, she thought, her irritation growing, he meant the sport of capturing her as his bride. Maybe actual hunting with his pack of hounds too, as he was sometimes hired to do, but definitely chasing her.

Would he never stop? Why did he fool himself so? Sadness for him sifted the anger bursting in her chest. But underneath both crawled that frightening tug that made her want to please her old friend, one of the few who cared about her. Even now she could see the laugh lines about his eyes from jokes they'd shared, knew of the callouses on his hands and how they'd helped her family at times. Hadn't he always been kind, until he grew tired of her refusals? He'd be kind again if she married him.

Belinda clutched her shawl tighter about her shoulders. He knew as well as she that she'd give in eventually. That no one else would have her. No one else cared. Wasn't that true?

No. No, it wasn't. That was the gray talking. That was what Gaspard had told her. She knew better than that. She'd never settle for someone whose character she couldn't trust. And there *were* others besides him who cared for her. She pinched the yellow silk of her shawl between her fingers like a lifeline to truths sometimes hard to believe. *You're a marvel, Belinda Lambton.* The gray tug lost its hold on her.

Regaining a poise worthy of the dress she wore, she said kindly, but firmly, "Gaspard, I'm sorry if I've hurt you—it was unintentional—but I will not marry you. I ask you to respect that and never speak of it again."

Grunting, Gaspard crossed his arms over his broad chest. "You sound like your high and mighty sisters—even look like them in that dress. Is it one of their castoffs? This is getting tiring, Bella pie."

You're telling me. Belinda rolled her eyes.

"Don't do that to me." Gaspard grabbed her elbow and pulled her to his side. "You're coming home with me."

"Is she?"

Belinda drew in a sharp breath, wishing she had a curse or mask or anything to hide behind. The protective edge in that new voice was almost as familiar as the blue eyes she knew she'd see if she turned. *Curses upon curses.* She could take care of this herself. Must she be doubly embarrassed by *him* helping?

Gaspard spun around, forcing her around likewise. She

took the opportunity to kick him just above his ankle and pull away.

"She belongs to me and is no concern of yours," he growled fiercely, despite his list to the side from her well-executed kick.

Belinda's indignation erupted in an inarticulate sputter that quickly died in the flames of embarrassment as she noted that Robert wasn't alone. Two soldiers flanked him.

That made three men with hands on their swords because of her.

Fortunately, Gaspard could count that high.

His stance lost some of its fight. The biggest, toughest man in the village was cowed.

Well, almost cowed.

Close enough. It was a new sight, and oh, Belinda loved it. She stepped pertly to Robert's side. "Please excuse him," she said. "He's an old acquaintance who thinks I need help getting home. But he must understand that I *don't* need help and I have *no* intention of going home until my father's there to greet me." She lifted her chin in defiance of whatever comeback Gaspard would give, but of course, the surly butcher wasn't listening to her but ineffectively trying to glare down Robert.

Robert raised an eyebrow, clearly unimpressed, and Belinda's heart gave a painful twist at the sense of something missing in that expression—fur, lots of almond-colored to deep-brown fur around those blue, blue eyes.

"I don't think King Patrick would approve of anyone *owning* another," Robert said icily. "That's not done in this kingdom, so I would refrain from making claims of that sort." He offered Belinda his arm, and she took it. "You needn't worry about getting the lady home. I will make sure she is safe."

Belinda's smile faltered but soon swept back into its

proper curve. Somehow, she fancied that Robert would gracefully accept her refusal to be escorted home.

"I'll see you soon, Belinda." A moment of steely glares passed before Gaspard's words escaped his clamped jaw. He scowled his displeasure at her, glowered at the three men, then stalked away.

"Not for three weeks, until my father's home," she called after him. And maybe not even then, if she could help it. She'd see her father, her few true friends, but not him. "Give my regards to your aunt and uncle."

Gaspard soon lost himself among the men and women walking the street, freeing Belinda from her need for company. She made to step away from Robert, but he stayed her with a light touch to her arm. He dismissed the soldiers, and she braced for the sight of those unnerving eyes as he turned back to her.

"Would you walk with me, Miss Lambton?"

She nodded, and he guided her slowly down the street. It was dusty and the flowers in the window boxes had withered and been cut back, but there was still an air of respectability about the village that made her encounter with Gaspard all the more humiliating. "All that wasn't necessary, Robert, but thank you. It saved me from the added indignity of having to drag Gaspard off the street after I knocked him senseless."

Robert's lips quirked, and he coughed suspiciously. *He wouldn't have a ghastly, toothy smile.* Belinda scolded her foolish thoughts and schooled her expression to prevent any unnecessary smiles of her own.

"I'm happy to have saved you that embarrassment, Miss Lambton. But I must confess, I was pleased to have an excuse to speak with you. Seeing you was an unexpected pleasure." He paused, his expression one of eager expectation, and a careful hope, that puzzled her.

She smiled uncertainly at him. "I am happy to see you again too, Robert."

He waited, and when she said no more, the hopeful look dimmed. He started them walking again, past a dressmaker and a baker. Where was the post office?

"Did—did someone send you to find me, Miss Lambton?" he asked at last.

"No," she said, startled. Wait. She took in his height and build again. Was *he* the man Lyndon met in the village that day it was storming? It would make sense. Could he give Beast's parents the letter for her?

"Oh." His shoulders slumped, his brows furrowing. She didn't like that defeated look on him. What was his connection to Beast? Her nose itched.

"Do you always travel this ... way?"

"Sometimes. I do not travel so easily as some, however." His face twisted into that expression of near-hate he'd given Lucrezia as he'd tugged on his ear the previous day, then sank into one of hurt. "Sometimes I try to meet up with an old friend, but our paths never seem to cross."

Intentionally not, if she knew that fur-ball coward of a friend of his. Yes, Robert would help her. "Perhaps he's an earlier riser than you expect," she said drily, considering how she should broach the subject of the letter. Directly talking about curses was tricky.

Robert huffed. "It wouldn't surprise me. He can be anything he believes he needs to be. But I must honor that, I guess."

That lump called a conscience rose with a vengeance in Belinda, still miffed from her earlier dismal of it. "There are times to force change, aren't there?" she asked.

"Yes. Sometimes it's necessary." He gave her a questioning look. "But it doesn't always work out well."

Belinda looked away, his eyes too familiar to be comfortable just then.

"I suppose sensible people have reasons for what they do," he continued, "though I must confess I sometimes find their actions difficult to justify."

Had she a right to force Beast to give up his curse? As Gaspard tried to force her to marry him, to allow him to look after her? He would claim good reasons for his actions and his disregard of her will. She claimed breaking Beast's curse was for the best. Beast claimed keeping it was for the best. Hadn't he told Lyndon, *It's better this way?*

"You think your friend sensible?" she asked.

A sad laugh escaped Robert. "'Undoubtedly, yes' is my initial response, but I begin to wonder. He may yet be—in all ways, or in every aspect save one." His voice hardened. "I am, in general, the latter: sensible in all save one." A faint hint of color rose in his cheeks. He added hurriedly, "At least, I strive to be sensible and honorable in all. So does he. Or he did." Robert shook his head. "I wish I knew," he said quietly.

"Is Lucrezia around?" Belinda asked, almost without thinking about it.

Undoubtedly, yes, Robert had said. The words knotted around her heart, warred there, and won. She would not force Beast's change. And especially not through deception.

How could she feel both better and worse for the same decision? Was it not for the best—for everyone—if he gave up his curse?

It wouldn't be better for you—you'd lose him.

I don't have him now and don't want him!

Belinda shut her heart against both ridiculous notions and unscrupulous uncurse plans.

If Robert gave any indication of surprise at her question concerning Lucrezia, it was lost to Belinda's battle with herself.

She looked up only in time to see him glance over his shoulder, brows drawn. She got a sense the young man wore that expression of concern and wariness far too often, and she pitied him.

"Not that I'm aware of," he said as he faced Belinda again, his gaze narrowing on her. "You're very perceptive, Miss Lambton."

Ignoring the hint of question in his statement, Belinda said, "Please don't be offended when I say I hope she isn't. I don't want her to be jealous, seeing us walking together like this." With a teasing smile, she briefly lifted their linked arms. "A red cheek would clash with the dress I'm wearing today."

He laughed. "I don't think *jealous* would be the word for what she feels regarding me." Amusement quickly turned to scorn, then dimmed as his eyes dulled in a far away look. His free hand rubbed something under his tunic, some manly version of a locket, Belinda suspected. *Is there someone you wish would be jealous of you? Someone Lucrezia's hold over you keeps you from?* The poor man was in some ways as cursed as Beast. Belinda prayed he'd soon be freed too.

They walked aimlessly past several shops before Robert shook off his melancholy, a look of hope suddenly burning in his gaze—and it was directed at her.

Her heart sank. Did the clouds blotting out the sky on gray days feel as despicable as she did in that moment? His hope was misplaced, if it was in her. She wouldn't be mailing the letter. She couldn't break Beast's curse. Not that way anyway.

Perhaps sensing her discomfort, Robert asked her of her errand in town and her father's journey, then treated her to lunch at the local hotel, proving himself an agreeable companion all the while.

An hour later, he walked Belinda outside the village to her horse, wished her a good day, and saw her ride safely away.

Not far into the woods, Marigold gave a nicker of pleasure.

"Where the devil have you been?" Beast practically jumped out of the bushes. If Marigold hadn't given her a warning, Belinda would have jumped too and been tempted to throw something at Beast. The scoundrel fell into step beside them. Marigold nuzzled his shoulder.

Ordering her heart to calm, her guilty expression to hide itself, Belinda lifted her chin. "Out for a ride, as I told you. I mailed a letter to my home—to my father, in case he arrives early—and another to some friends. I told them I was safe."

Beast rubbed Marigold's muzzle absently, saving his attention to glare at Belinda. "That's all very well, but you didn't bloody well say you were going off the castle grounds *all the way to the village.*"

A grin forced its way past Belinda's guard. "Am I a prisoner that I should stay inside them? I wasn't looking for *her*, so I broke no command that I knew. And I hadn't intended to stay gone so long."

Beast looked ready to argue, then, as if thinking better of it, said sulkily, "No." A limp disrupted his gait, and he said softly, "I was afraid you'd left for good, without saying goodbye."

Belinda swallowed a lump in her throat. *I wouldn't leave you, not without saying goodbye.* "You used the mirror to find me, didn't you?"

"You know about that?" he asked in surprise. Then, sighing heavily, he added, "Of course, you know about that."

"If you'd given me a proper tour of the castle, I wouldn't have had to take myself on one. I find interesting things when I take myself on tours."

Beast's huff was strong enough to startle Marigold. She nickered, and he patted her shoulder. "You're practically a spy, Belinda Lambton."

"You should talk."

Beast made no response.

"I mean it," she said. "You *should* talk. I'd love to listen."

"No."

"But—"

"I'm the strong and silent type, Miss Lambton. You should know that by now. Your pleas fall on deaf ears."

Belinda's retort died in a hiss of shock as another person jumped out of the bushes. This one with a cocked pistol and a face that left her wondering if the pistol was a scare tactic or something beyond that. Her gaze jumped from Gaspard to his gun to Beast, and her mind thundered a warning that left her trembling. *Gaspard the hunter. Beast, furry, mounted trophy.*

Belinda jumped off Marigold, shouting, "Don't hurt him, Gaspard! He's just a man." She darted in front of Beast and threw her arms out as if to shield him. Beast stumbled back in shock, barely keeping from running into Belinda.

Gaspard rolled his eyes, though he didn't lower his gun. "Of course, he's a man. I'm no idiot. It's that guy from the village with some crazy cat-bear costume on."

"Incompetent enchantress," Beast muttered under his breath as he moved beside Belinda, who tried ineffectively to keep him behind her.

"People have been asking questions about you, Belinda," Gaspard said, waving his pistol at Beast. "Now that this fellow's bullies aren't with him, you're coming with me."

Beast's head snapped up. A growl rumbled his chest. "Miss Lambton—"

"Goes where she chooses." Splaying her fingers against Beast's chest to hold him back, Belinda stepped in front of him again. "I'm working with a traveling troupe of players while my father's gone, and there's nothing you can do about it." Once again, Belinda raised her chin in proud defiance only to find Gaspard not paying her any attention. He was sizing up Beast. Beast, looking as supercilious as only a cat can, stared back at him as if sizing up Gaspard had taken so little time he was now bored.

Men. She was about ready to use the scare tactic she'd brought along in case of meeting Lucrezia.

Gaspard focused on her again, narrowing his eyes as his gaze traced her hand to Beast's chest. "Is there anything between you and this ..." Gaspard jerked his chin at Beast, a sneer replacing any pronoun for her true friend.

Belinda jerked her hand away from Beast's chest. "Of course I'm not in love with him!" she snapped. "He's a—he insists on wearing this ridiculous costume all the time!"

Beast started and gave her a sideways glance, his eyes wide. Gaspard reddened.

Belinda bit her lip. She may have been a bit too adamant in her response. But she was only trying to avoid a very unfair fight!

Gaspard un-cocked his pistol and slid it into his belt. "Take off the suit, cat-beast. We can fight here."

"The suit stays on." Beast crossed his arms as Gaspard removed his jacket. "I wouldn't put you at a disadvantage by taking it off."

"Beast," Belinda hissed, grabbing ahold of his furry but very muscular bicep. "What are you thinking? You can't do this. You know better!"

He cocked his head to look at her, his expression one of complete confidence. Her heart did that strange flip-flop. Blast blue-eyed men and beasts!

With a growl of her own, Belinda lunged forward, seized Gaspard's pistol, tossed it into the bushes, shoved Gaspard after it, then leapt onto Marigold and galloped away.

They wanted to fight over her? Fine. But they'd have to catch her first.

It didn't take Beast long. He caught up with them as

Marigold leapt over a fallen limb. He landed on all fours beside them, keeping pace. It didn't seem to bother Marigold that her master was racing her, which made Belinda wonder if Beast had raced his horses before.

So much for her impression of an indolent Beast. He'd apparently managed to fool even his enchantress.

"I'm not in that much of a hurry to get home," Beast huffed, "and it is a ... *huff* ... lovely afternoon. ... *huff* ... Do you think you ... *huff* ... could slow your pace?"

Gaspard was nowhere in sight, so Belinda reined in Marigold. Beast helped her dismount, then led them to a hidden glade on the castle side of the stream and settled Belinda on a moss-cushioned rock. He let Marigold free to graze, then stretched out on the ground beside Belinda. They sat there quietly, Belinda listening to the birds and breathing in all the earthy scents, simply delighting in nature, Beast doing the same, though his gaze strayed to Belinda more than to the birds flittering about.

As the sun began to set, Beast offered Belinda his paw and motioned for home. As they left the glade, Belinda leading Marigold by the reins, Beast thumbed back toward the village, breaking Belinda's sense of peace. "He's the reason you followed me home that day, isn't he?"

She lowered her gaze to the dust-covered hem of her apricot gown. "Yes." She added in a murmur, "Arrogant jackanapes. Thinking he can order everyone about. *Home, Belinda. Marry me, Belinda.*" She huffed. Beast asking her in concealed politeness was bad enough, but Gaspard's unrelenting insistence and barely concealed threats were too much.

Beast chuckled. Piqued, Belinda spun around to poke him in the chest. "You think that's funny?"

He shrugged as he caught her hand. "I can't fault his sense in them where you're concerned. I could think of much less reasonable things to insist on."

"He's not above doing more than insist." The comment escaped as a twinge of unease shimmied up her spine.

"What?" Beast said sharply, his expression hardening in a dangerous way. His hand tightened around hers, large and furry and clawed, yet somehow safe.

And that made her heart ache.

But Belinda Lambton wasn't the type to suffer from things like heartaches. Those were for other women, not for her.

"He might try anyway," she said, forcing spirit into her voice as she freed her hand. She poked Beast on his velvet-coated chest. "And don't think *you* can order *me* around. I pack a gun, and I'm not above rapping you upside the head with it if you get bossy."

"You can't reach my head."

"When you're cowering on the ground trying to avoid my wild shots, I can."

He arched a furry eyebrow, then patted her on the head and strode past her. "I'm returning to the castle, Miss Lambton. If you don't wish to get left out with the wolves and the Gaspards, then you'd better step lively."

Half a dozen feet away, he looked back. Belinda's glare had melted into a grin. She flattened it out and tugged Marigold's reins, starting her forward. She took Beast's proffered arm as she reached him. He shortened his strides and she lengthened hers to match, and they walked on together.

CHAPTER 12

L yndon wasted no time in giving Belinda both a hug and a scolding. Belinda accepted both, the former as her pleasure and the latter as her due, then excused herself and returned to her room. There was someone she wanted to talk to.

"Lady Violetta." She paced in front of her vanity and repeated the call. "Lady Violetta."

Stealing a glance in the vanity mirror, she picked up the silver hairbrush to give her hands something to do and tweaked her clean gown—one of her finest. Somehow, she thought it might make the enchantress more amenable if her delicate sense of fashion weren't violated by Belinda's appearance. "Lady Violetta," she called again. "I need you."

She jumped but easily stifled her scream when a burst of vibrant hues of blue and sparkling white resolved behind her into the enchantress. The latter was dressed in a six-foot-round dress that made her look like the goddess-like centerpiece of an azure fountain.

Belinda blinked, momentarily dazzled.

"Yes, dear?" Lady Violetta nodded graciously as she took

in Belinda's gown. Her self-satisfied expression indicated she was still basking in Belinda's evident awe. Which was probably well for Belinda.

Belinda crossed her arms and leveled the enchantress with her most dissatisfied glare. "Will you remove the daily proposal requirement for Beast?"

Dragging her gaze from Belinda's slippers, Lady Violetta cocked an eyebrow. "Why should I?"

Belinda narrowed her eyes. "Lucrezia Marblue ... and ropes embedded with glass and rock."

Lady Violetta stumbled back, barely remembering to magically whip up a chair before attempting sitting on air. "Lucrezia," she muttered.

"Well?" Belinda said a moment later, tapping her toes as a reminder that she was awaiting an answer. "Do I need to tell Beast's *parents* about it?"

The play of colors, like a rainbow in mist, about Lady Violetta's dress poofed out. "I see your point," she said, nodding as she spoke, "but I'm afraid I can't." She shrugged, somehow making the gesture look elegant. "Once an addendum is added to a curse, I can't just do away with it. You know no magical wedding will suddenly take place if someone accepts him. Nothing will happen, I think ..."

"Only that Beast will feel honor-bound to marry the one who accepts him. I won't ask him to give up his honor or to marry someone like *that woman*. You must do something."

"I can't. I'm bound by the curse's rules too."

Belinda stifled a curse of a different kind. "Then can you change the rotation of the villages?"

She shrugged again. "I could try?"

"Then try."

Lady Violetta nodded, her eyes on her lap, her gaze constantly shifting as if watching something in her thoughts. Her violet eyes snapped back up to Belinda, startling her.

"You wouldn't know when your village returns. Or do you wish me to keep it at its original rotation, six weeks after you arrived?"

"Keep it the same."

"Are you sure? You seem hesitant."

"*Keep it.* But change it by a day so *she* won't show up. And I need a copy of the new circuit."

"You're very demanding today."

"I'm trying to do what you asked me to." Or at least keep Beast safe until he gave up his curse, if ever.

Lady Violetta settled into her chair and rested her hands in her lap. Belinda didn't really care to have the enchantress studying her, but she refused to look away.

"How are you and Beast getting along?" Lady Violetta asked at length.

Belinda mimicked Lady Violetta's elegant shrug, her chest tightening. "Well enough."

"Your cheeks are pink." She cocked her head to study her. "You like him."

"He saved my life," Belinda snapped. "Of course I *like* him. In a way."

"He saved your life?" Lady Violetta started. "Perhaps I should reconsider that dress, after all."

"Oh no, you don't. I—I wouldn't be fit to marry him."

"You would if you were wearing one of my dresses."

"Do they enchant people to approve of you?" Belinda said with distaste. "Turn you into a proper lady?"

"Don't look at me that way, young lady. I am not one of *those* fairy godmothers."

Belinda tightened her grip on the hairbrush. *Or was she?*

"But," Lady Violetta added after a significant pause, "they might not be as vehement in their objections as they might otherwise be, at least until after the wedding, at which point it will be too late and they must learn to deal with it."

"I'd prefer our families to like one another. And be of similar social standing."

Lady Violetta shrugged again. She looked down at her nails, smoothing the painted tip of one with her fingernail.

"Did you mean earlier," Belinda said carefully, stepping closer, "that there are other fairy godmothers who might stoop to giving their favorites the power to control another?"

"Yes. Though it's not allowed officially."

She took another step. "Are you familiar with a wealthy man of military bearing called Robert, who's associated with this beautiful-to-look-at, mean-as-a-snake Lucrezia?"

Lady Violetta's eyes flared wide in stunning violet, like the violet of a sunset cloud. It was tinged with the pink of her eye shadow. "Why do you ask?"

"I take that as a yes. I suspect Lucrezia has some kind of enchanted control over him. He seems very nice, and I don't like her messing with him. And I don't want her to use him against Beast."

Lady Violetta became very still.

Belinda stalked forward. "*You* didn't grant her any favors, did you?"

The floor between Belinda and Lady Violetta expanded.

"Now, dear," Lady Violetta said warily, holding her hand up, palm out, though Belinda quickly realized she'd never cross that stretched stretch of floor. "We're required to do pro-bono work as fairy godmothers to stay licensed in the Guild of Practicing Enchanters. And if I did act a little hastily in choosing a recipient for a good deed the night before the deadline—the girl was crying so pathetically and showed such excellent fashion sense, and I didn't have time to thoroughly research her—you can hardly blame me. I had to grant a wish by midnight. It wasn't until later that it occurred to me to be suspicious that she had a spell picked out for me. She said her steward was mismanaging her estate and she was powerless to stop him on her own. With a control spell, she could manage what was her own. Fairy godmothers aren't normally expected, you know."

"Fortunately, she got *you*," Belinda said sourly, "because the spell was botched and put Robert under her influence instead of the one she surely intended it for—Beast."

Lady Violetta winced. "After this case, I shall retire and devote myself to fashion," she murmured. "Well," she said, rising, "I'll see about the new kingdom tour plan. Do keep doing whatever you're doing. I think it's having an effect, though I'm not exactly sure what kind."

"Wait. Will Lucrezia be able to get a copy of the new plan?"

"It's possible. I must give it to Beast's family, after all."

"Which means Lucrezia will make Robert get it for her."

"I could request he not have access to it."

"I'm not so sure that would stop her."

Lady Violetta sighed as if in agreement, then raised her wand, which was showing signs of a building glow. "Take care, my dear. I'll see what I can do." The wand brightened.

"Wait—just once more." Belinda held out her hand. "Thank you for coming, Lady Violetta." She smiled meekly. "And for being willing to help."

Lady Violetta's eyes widened, but then she smiled in return, a simple, genuine smile. "I think," she said, "that *when* he asks the question and is answered affects everything." She gave Belinda a look meant to tell her something, then disappeared.

Belinda slumped into a chair. A new route would only help for so long. What else could Beast do? And how could she alert him to the new plan without revealing how much she knew? Her stomach knotted at the thought of him knowing she knew Lady Violetta and thus about the proposals. He likely suspected already, but the longer they could pretend she didn't understand him, the better. As long as it was pretend, she didn't have to give an answer. Not a real one, anyway. A tacit rejection through silence wouldn't cause either pain.

"BEAST," Belinda addressed him halfway through the main course and a discourse on favorite composers, "you need a chaperone for your daily ramblings. I don't think your parents would approve of the way you harass the women you meet while out and about. If I'm with you, I'm sure I won't dream."

A leg of lamb halfway to his mouth, Beast froze, then blinked. "No." The leg of lamb resumed its path.

"Beast," Belinda said halfway through dessert and a conversation on the best cheese base for fondue, "do you have any relatives among the werewolves? Because someone might mistake you for one and impale you with something deadly sharp and silver unless you have someone with you to vouch for your good character."

"No."

"Beast," Belinda began halfway to the library and halfway through a discussion of the superiority of Shakespearean tragedies or comedies, "do you——"

"No."

"You know where this is going, don't you?"

"Yes, and the answer is *no.*"

With her sunniest grin, which wasn't difficult to conjure, she turned her face to Beast's. "At least I got you to give one affirmative."

Beast's furry face shifted, and he limped, a slight list to the right. Belinda, her arm through his, compensated.

"Are your ankles healing?"

"Yes, the limp was ... something else, I think." His face shifted again, to a thoughtful, almost frowning line of fur. He didn't resume his support in favor of tragedies. "I meant what I said about her," he said as they reached the library door.

Belinda's jaw ticked, but she forced a smile. "How about a deal? If she doesn't show tomorrow, then I can go with you? I'd rather walk with you than be forced into sudden slumber every time you go out. It's most disconcerting. Not to mention rude to whoever I'm talking with."

"You talk to so many people here," Beast said drily. "And the answer is still no. She undoubtedly will show tomorrow, so I don't understand why you'd even suggest—" Beast stopped and spun Belinda to face him, his eyes bright and all hers. "Belinda! What do you know?"

Belinda. How many times had he slipped and called her that today?

It might have been the two furry paws clasping her shoulders like a heavy stole, but Belinda felt warm to her toes. "Well, you know ... this is an enchanted castle, and things happen and well ..." She pulled a neatly rolled parchment tied with a rainbow-colored ribbon from her sleeve. "Here."

Her heart did a painful twist as Beast released her shoulders and took the parchment. *Honesty is always best. No relationship can thrive without it.* Her father's words brought a stab of regret. She wanted to be honest with Beast, but didn't think Lady Violetta would approve. Any more than Belinda wanted to face Beast giving a blatant proposal. Or have him think she lied her way here, that the enchantress sent her.

"The schedule's changed," he said, dumbfounded, then his face broke into that ghastly grin. "It's changed!" A spark of lighthearted happiness lit his eyes as he stepped forward, his arms out. He froze and backed away, still beaming, but not as brightly. He offered her his arm. "To the library, Miss Lambton? *Our* schedule hasn't changed. Even the length of your stay is practically the same."

She took his arm and let him lead her with a tug of regret.

She was almost positive that, had he been a man, he would have picked her up and spun her around in a dancing kind of joy, but the beast kept him from it. She was also almost positive that the recognition of that need for restraint didn't do more than faintly dim his joy.

But even as an uncursed man, it'd be better if he didn't, and he knew it as surely as she.

"You know this is likely only a temporary reprieve, don't you?" she said, fighting a ridiculous sadness trying to creep into her voice.

"Yes, but I'm grateful for even that. I will change my routine, go at different times of the day than previously. I had grown too predictable, and I—"

"And you enjoyed the challenge of the escape, playing the wily fox."

"Yes," Beast said, "how well you know me, Belinda!" He added quietly as he settled her into her wingback chair, "But the game is too serious now."

Belinda hesitated and studied the fire, focusing on each dart and retreat of the flames. "Will you not give it up?" she asked quietly.

He was silent a moment. "No," he answered softly. Belinda felt he'd looked many places during that long moment, including her. "We are back," he added with false cheerfulness, "to our earlier conversation, it seems, a series of no's. Come, let us read. I believe you'll approve of what I've selected."

Though the familiar pressure of gray settled on her chest, Belinda eyed the title, then flicked her hand dismissively as she raised her chin. "Your copy of *Pride and Prejudice* is not worn enough to suit me, sir."

"Ah! You desire to read for Lady Catherine?" He bowed low and said with affected solemnity, "May I compliment your taste in literature, architecture, music, and everything else, your ladyship?"

"And tell, with utmost gravity, the mother of any single young lady of the charm and beauty of her daughters?"

He bowed again. "Mr. Collins would tell it so much better than I."

Her laughter as she accepted the volume rang out surprisingly full, though it came from a chest that felt empty. Beast must have thought it full though, for he gave her one of those ghastly, ivory grins.

"Very well then," she said, her heart twisting at a sudden image of a grin on an unscarred, Robert-like face. "I accept your request. What scenes are we to read?" By which question, she meant, "Which proposal?"

It was to be Mr. Collins's. Her heart beat easier. That would be a proposal she could enjoy rejecting.

CHAPTER 13

"Beast," Belinda began the next morning as they met leaving their rooms, "it's a lovely day and—"

"No."

"You need to expand your vocabulary."

"And you your desires."

"I was only going to comment on how lovely a walk *in the garden* would be. Before I suddenly fall unconscious at an inconvenient time." She could only hope the change in schedule threw Lucrezia off, but Belinda wasn't going to count on it for long. There was more than one way to skin a beast down to his human hide—and she'd figure that out—so there had to be more than one way to protect that hide from huntresses. Belinda wouldn't be around dreaming for long, only three more weeks. Who would look after him then?

"You're not going to fall asleep while I am here."

"I know, which is why I want you walking *with* me. I wouldn't want to risk hitting the pavement."

"I'll let you know when I'm going Beyond the Gates from now on, how's that?"

"That's acceptable. Garden?" It was a lovely place for thinking. And she'd left something for him there.

He offered her his arm. "Your wish is my command, my lady."

"You know a person so inclined could take advantage of a comment like that, right?"

"Which is why I would only say it to one too wise to be so inclined," he replied with a slight threat in his tone that didn't match the teasing glint in his eyes.

"I thought as much," she said, pretending to shrink back in fear.

He tugged her back to his side, and they walked on, Belinda covertly guiding until they neared the fountain at the center of the garden. A pillowcase-sized stack of books, their gilded titles mostly unreadable to Belinda with or without her reading spell, formed a colorful addition to the fountain's base.

Belinda cleared her throat as Beast spun to stare at her. "I was afraid of acquiring a fine," she said, not quite meeting his gaze, "so I thought I'd better return them. I find myself too lazy to diligently study *all* of these languages. I must admit I miss the lovely foreign accents you managed when you asked your rhetorical questions when I first came."

"Thank you, Belinda," he said with feeling. His gaze darted away from her, and he began speaking in a tired, sad voice, "You've deduced so much that I'm sure you—"

"Just don't insult me in any language but our own," she cut in hastily. "Rhetorical questions only, mind."

"I'm not going to insult you in any language, Belinda," he said firmly, a hint of scolding in his tone as he locked gazes with her.

Not for the first time in his and Lyndon's presence, even Robert's, Belinda felt as if she'd stepped into another realm, one of kindness too great for her.

"Lyndon and I go hunting today," he said after a long moment, looking away to the fountain. He led her slowly around it and started back toward the castle.

"I'll stay inside then," she said quickly.

"You don't wish to join us? Lyndon mentioned that you hunt. I would protect you."

Yes, Gaspard and his uncle had taught her.

Gaspard who thought Beast was wearing a costume.

"Another time perhaps," she answered absently. She'd had an epiphany, and her lips showed it.

Beast crouched to study her face. "Miss Lambton, that smile worries me."

The smile brightened, as did her eyes. "Does it? Beasts have a much wider range of emotions than I thought possible. I assumed worry was a human phenomenon. But do go on. I know how to entertain myself now."

Beast's expression, when he left her in the library, was more than a trifle concerned.

THERE WAS no lady in the dreams that morning. That evening, after Beast told Belinda of the hunt and asked about her afternoon, she merely grinned with gleeful mischief.

"Wyjdziesz za mnie?" Beast asked as they parted for the night. Belinda smiled and wished him a goodnight.

The next day was much the same. In the morning, Beast asked his question, and Belinda smiled. After the dream, in which no lady appeared, Belinda cloistered herself away at her little desk in the library. Late that evening, however, she put away her quill with a confident finality.

"I'M BACK, BELINDA," Beast called through her door the next morning. "Are you awake yet? I wondered if you'd like to go for a run? I mean, I run and you ride Marigold."

Belinda yanked the door open with such suddenness Beast started and scowled at her. Easing his scowl into merely a raised eyebrow, he said drily, "I see you're up." He held out his arm as she joined him in the hallway. "In that case, good morning, Belinda. *Willst du mich heiraten?*"

Eyes bright and smiling merrily, Belinda shut the door behind her and slipped her arm though his. "*Willst du mich heiraten,* Beast?" Their arms linked, she bounced back against Beast when he didn't move with her forward step. She glanced up at him. He was staring ahead in a wide-eyed daze. Laughing quietly, she tugged him forward, and he came, shaking his head and limping.

"You should be careful what you say in a foreign language, Belinda."

She winked at him. "I know. Come. I have something for you, but it will wait until after our outing." She eyed his leg, her brow furrowed. "If you're up to it?"

He followed her gaze to his right leg as it gave slightly with each step. Seemingly rallying his wits, he straightened and set his jaw. "I'm up for it." His walk regained its prowess and power.

Which he needed for the race. Belinda hadn't always been a poor peasant. She'd lived long enough as a wealthy merchant's daughter to learn to ride quality horses, and Marigold was quality.

"You know, if you'd practiced more, you might have won that lap." Belinda cooled down Marigold by walking her in a circle around Beast, who'd chosen to collapse on the leaves.

"I am *not* ... *huff* ... walking on ... *huff* ... all fours as my ... *huff* ... normal form of ... *huff* ... perambulation."

Belinda shrugged. "Don't expect to win then. Not when I'm riding anyway."

Beast snorted. "Next time, I'll tackle you and ... *huff* ... then continue the race one on one with Marigold."

"So you're not above frightening the horse to help you win? That's despicable."

"That's not—" Beast shook his head and gave up to laughter. When the laughter had eased, he pulled himself to his knees. "I'm glad you came, Belinda. Even if you're a bit crazy."

"Hey! I thought you said you wouldn't insult me!"

"Who said that was an insult?"

"It certainly sounded like—"

A bright light flared above them, and Belinda gasped as Marigold shied. Beast leapt up and grabbed Marigold's reins. Additional flares lit the air and were accompanied by hisses.

Belinda slid off Marigold and scooted closer to Beast as he watched the sky. "That's not a meteor shower, is it?" she asked.

He shook his head. "Someone's testing the magical boundary. With arrows, I think. I felt someone trying to get in earlier." There was a smugness to his expression that eased the snarls in her stomach.

"Are you sure it's not someone from your family trying to get your attention?"

"No, they know how to signal for entry, and I'd sense them."

The tangles won out again. "You think it's her?"

"Possibly. I'm going to the tower. You find Lyndon and tell him." His eyes as he focused on her held more than his usual air of authority. "Don't leave the grounds."

He dropped to all fours and raced away before Belinda could protest the absurdity of her leaving the shield of Beast's territory when someone was using arrows against it. Deciding to take Beast's command as a sign of his care rather than a lack of confidence in her sense, she mounted Marigold. They followed after Beast at a slower gait.

Belinda paced with Lyndon in the library for an hour before they settled in with books they tried in vain to read. Beast joined them just before dinner.

"Well?" she and Lyndon asked together.

Beast shrugged and settled into his chair with a longing look at the tray of tea and biscuits. Belinda poured him a cup of tea.

"I'd forgotten how close today's village is to Marblue," he said. "It's nothing to worry about."

Belinda narrowed her eyes at him to warn him against dissembling, but he gave her a toothy smile as he accepted the cup of tea and a biscuit. "You said you had something for me earlier, Belinda. Did I forfeit it by beating you back to the castle?"

"No, nor did you by losing the race." She gathered a stack of handwritten papers from her desk and held it out to Beast as Lyndon looked on inquiringly.

"I didn't realize you wrote," Beast said around his biscuit as he put down his tea and accepted the stack with interest. His eyes took on that *blue bird in a sky of clouds* look as his brows rose. He stole a glance at her before continuing to scan the pages. "I can see," he said as he straightened the stack, "that it's dangerous to leave you unattended, Miss Lambton. Lyndon, from now on, you're going to play chess with Miss Lambton, all day, every day."

"I only do half shifts on chess, Master. You'll have to take the afternoon one." Lyndon smiled mildly, craning to catch a glimpse of the papers from his chair on the other side of Belinda. Beast handed them off to him.

"Or she could go Beyond the Gate with me. I suppose that was the intention," Beast said with a significant look at her.

"I wouldn't want to intrude on your quiet meditations in the forest."

Beast huffed. "You may accompany me, if you wish, but if she shows up, you are to return to the castle without interacting with her. Understood?"

"I don't want anything to do with her." Belinda added in a mutter, "Unless it's to bloody her nose."

"Belinda ..."

"I wouldn't, don't worry. I don't agree with revenge. Besides, this is about *avoiding* her."

"How so?"

"*The Proposals of Pauline* by Miss Belinda Lambton." Lyndon cut off Belinda's answer, reading aloud with amusement in his tone. "Miss Pauline Diggle was by no means an attractive young woman. She was, in point of fact, plain. Her nose was too large, her teeth crooked, and her eyes, while passing fair in their color, were lost to notice due to the mocking tendency of the half-circle under her eyes to take on a purple hue. It was this purple-ness under the eyes, her parents were certain, that kept their daughter a maiden at the ancient age of twenty. Consequently, when by strange good fortune they saved a fairy from a potentially devastating (to the fairy's mind) entanglement with an *iron*wood tree, the grateful fairy granted them a wish, and they asked for her to help Pauline get married. And so it came to pass that Plain Pauline was blessed in such a way that every single man who met her felt inclined to propose to her, to the fright of the unsuspecting Pauline. Thus began the perilous adventures of Pauline Diggle."

Lyndon chuckled as he slid the first page to the back. Beast, on the other hand, leaned his head on his hand and rubbed his forehead. Belinda's face heated, but once again her answer was cut off by Lyndon.

"Let's see," he continued. "We have chases through the

shrubbery, balcony climbs, desperate disguises, episodes of hiding behind drapes, and general chaos in the court when the unsuspecting Pauline goes to work as a maid at the palace. Even an international incident." He gave a significant look at Beast. "And a pet bear at the palace who befriends the heroine. This is very clever, Miss Lambton, and possibly a solution to some of the, shall we say, undesirable acquaintances of ours?"

Beast glanced up, skepticism sharpening his expression. "How?"

"By hiding you and your predicament in plain sight," Belinda said before Lyndon could cut her off. "I propose a series of plays based on Pauline's adventures escaping proposals to be performed in each village. Now"—she held up her hand to forestall Beast's objections—"you don't have to perform. We can work together to make some of my ideas fit for public consumption—otherwise, food that should be consumed will end up on the players' faces. You'll hire troupes of players for each region the castle travels to, and you and I will go each day into town with a part of the troupe to advertise the traveling show. You'll wear a sign—one that drapes over your chest and back—that says 'Coming tonight *The Proposals of Pauline*' and that has various relevant phrases, like 'Daring Escapes,' 'Marry me!' and 'Will she ever say yes?' on it. You won't have to *say* anything. No one will bother to talk to you. There will be another actor or two with costumes made to match you for the actual shows. Gaspard thought you in costume. So will everyone else."

"You'll be guarded by a crowd, Master," Lyndon said, "and with the sign no one will—that is no one will be afraid of you and take you for a mindless creature."

"They don't take me for one now," Beast muttered, staring at the fire. He added quietly, "Just a fool human in a costume."

"It's just an idea in case your schedule gets figured out," Belinda said. "I leave in little more than two weeks and want to know that you'll be looked after when I'm not dreaming of you." She paused, her heart thumping so loudly she feared Beast would hear. "Unless ..."

"Unless you can think of another way to end that problem," Lyndon said with meaning.

Beast's head snapped up. "There is no other way. Not now." He and Lyndon scowled at one another until Lyndon sighed and looked away. Beast gave Belinda a quick glance, refusing to meet her eye before turning to the fire, his paw clenching the chair arm.

Belinda rubbed her chest, where, if she were the kind of woman prone to suffer such afflictions, would be an ache. But Belinda was too tough and too sensible for such a thing. "Why don't we go to the music room tonight? You can teach me that song you promised. I have little time left here. We should make the most of it."

"AND DOES the prince ever propose to Pauline?" Lyndon asked the next day with a sly smile as he, Beast, and Belinda completed their second play, the one where Pauline narrowly escapes the passionate proposals of the smitten Count de Dimwitty by taking a shortcut down the stairs and across the great hall by swinging from a chandelier lowered for cleaning. "She is working at the palace, after all."

Fortunately, Belinda had prepared an answer to that inevitable question. "Naturally, you'd think that, but the fairy knew better than to include the prince among the susceptible," she said quickly, focusing intently on the script.

Beast cleared his throat with a scathing look at Lyndon. "That's right, Lyndon. *Royalty* are naturally immune to spells."

"Curses in particular," Lyndon said drily.

"Yes." Beast took the pile of papers from Belinda, tapped them into a neat stack, and laid them on the table beside his chair. Firelight gleamed against a bit of tooth exposed by a smile. "This has proven entertaining," he said after a moment, "even if I plan to never need the plays."

"I'm glad it's worth something," Belinda said lightly as she rose stiffly from her desk and stretched.

"Personally, I was hoping for fame as a playwright." Lyndon covered a yawn with his hand as he rose. "Good night. I'll see you both in the morning." He kissed Belinda on the cheek, patted Beast on the shoulder, then left.

Entreating Belinda to leave the mess on her desk for the morning, Beast took her arm and escorted her as usual to her room. Belinda steeled herself as they stopped before her door. He hadn't asked her his usual question yet, and that unnerved her, though she couldn't fathom why.

He took her hand as she released his arm. "I had a pleasant evening, Belinda. Good night and ... *shte se omŭzhish li za men?*"

"Good night, Beast." Smiling tightly, Belinda turned for the door and found herself unable to reach it, her hand still held in Beast's. She turned slowly back around. Beast watched her expectantly, his eyes twinkling like blue fireflies. He twitched her hand gently, waiting.

Belinda swallowed. Curse the butterflies in her stomach and the ache in her chest.

"*Shte se omŭzhish li za men?*" she said quietly, and spun toward her door. "Good night, Beast." But once again her hand didn't follow. She turned reluctantly back to the light of Beast's eyes. His toothy, teasing smile only frightened the butterflies into a gossamer knot.

"No, Belinda," he said, stepping a little closer. "If *you're* going to ask, you must say, '*Shte se ozhenish li za men?*'" He lifted her hand as if to kiss it, but gently squeezing it instead, he bowed and backed away. His eyes danced merrily as he released her. "Good night, Miss Lambton. Dream of me tomorrow."

Her heart thumping foolishly, Belinda fled into her room and fell back against the closed door, her hand clenching the twisted, hideous knob. If that man weren't already cursed, she'd ...

Her throat tightened. She'd never have met him and would never have been permitted to speak with him.

She touched a hand to her burning cheek. Blast gray and pink. She'd not give in to either.

CHAPTER 14

The next few weeks passed quickly, and pleasantly Belinda told herself as she packed the yellow shawl into the small valise Beast insisted she take with her.

But they were a failure.

Beast was as stubborn as she, but while he had the right to keep his curse, she had no right to force its end. She smiled wanly as she drew a cloak over her shoulders. Her parting shot was in her pocket: Beast's letter to his parents and a note from herself begging him to send the former to his parents. She'd give it to him in place of a goodbye. A knock sounded on the door, and she forced her thoughts to her father, which quickly yielded the happy smile she wanted as she reached for the door, where Beast waited.

Mid-morning, he had walked peacefully through familiar woods. Now he was ready to escort her through the forest to the outskirts of the village, to see her safely off there.

"You know that if your father's not returning for some time," Lyndon said as he stood with her at the front door a few minutes later, "you're welcome to return. Please do."

"I know," Belinda said as she savored his fatherly embrace. The mirror had shown her father still traveling, but he'd have sent a message ahead to tell her when to expect him. Within a few days, she hoped.

Lyndon released her and tapped her valise, with its copy of the castle's travel schedule, and, she suspected, traveling money. "Any time. And meet us back in the forest six weeks from now, so we can check on you."

She expressed her thanks with a kiss on his cheek. "Good-bye, Lyndon."

She handed her valise to Beast and took his arm, the velvet of his jacket soft under her fingers. No fur coat as a disguise this time.

They strolled through the forest, its limbs gray and bare compared to her last flight through it. Soon, the trees and rocks grew familiar and reminded Belinda of their first day together. They were hunted strangers then, but now? She smiled wryly. They were about the same ... She glanced up at Beast, her fingers tightening over his bicep as he looked down at her as he spoke, sharing a story with her. *Not quite the same.* Not yet, anyway. Soon enough, they'd be strangers again.

As if familiar with the forest himself, Beast stopped beside the old tree with a hollow hidden behind evergreen shrubs, an appropriate place for Beast to disappear from her life.

Belinda swallowed the lump in her throat and considered her letter as she accepted her valise from Beast.

"I'll wait here," he said, crossing his arms as he leaned against the husk of the tree. "You can come back and let me know about your father."

Grateful for the reprieve, Belinda nodded and quickened her steps toward the village.

It was a market town really, fair-sized, even boasting a mostly intact donjon at its center. The ancient stone keep towered above the houses and served as a reminder not to misbehave, lest one find oneself in its damp tower. It didn't deter many of the shopkeepers below it, however, from "small" sins like dishonest scales. Gaspard's butcher shop crouched in the tower's shadow, undeterred.

Though they had no reason to be intimidated by the tower, Belinda and her father's half-timber home was on the village's outskirts. She half expected to see Gaspard stalking about the place, leaving the work of his shop to his apprentice, as usual.

But the house and yard were empty. No Gaspard. No poultry and goats either. Belinda shook her head. The animals hadn't been taken care of so much as removed. So much for Lady Violetta's "taking care of everything."

Belinda unlocked the front door, then stepped back. The house was empty ... save for the odor of the vegetables and bread she'd left out thinking she'd be returning much earlier to use them. Wrinkling her nose as she made her way inside, she picked up the letters pushed under the door and set them on the kitchen table as she passed by. One letter had a familiar, masculine script, but she left it and hastily cleared away the evidence of her six weeks' neglect.

That done and the windows opened, she gathered her bright shawl to help drive away any threatening gray, and picked up her father's note. Her heart beat, her heart thumped in contradictory rhythms as she slid her fingernail under the seal, opened the letter, and read.

Three weeks. She had another three weeks. Why not one or five?

Belinda sank into a chair. She could stay and risk Gaspard for three weeks, or she could return to the castle for another six and leave her father a similar note: *Unavoidably detained but doing well. Three weeks until I'm home. Love.*

Her heart leapt. She had six more weeks with—

She sank further into her seat. She'd failed as a curse

breaker, and there was no other reason to return. Not really. She tugged at the fringe of her shawl. She could deal with Gaspard herself. She was strong enough for that now, though she'd honestly rather not have to.

But was dealing with him worth it, if she didn't have to? Maybe she could still do something about that curse breaking.

A knock on the front door sent her into the air, and it was only the recognition of the feminine lightness to the sound that brought her gaze from the back door, with its offer of escape, to the front.

"Heavens, Belinda." The pastor's wife bustled in as Belinda opened the door. "You could have told us you were going away *before* we'd worried ourselves sick for three weeks, and even then you only sent a letter! We assumed you went to your aunt's, but then we remembered you said she was away herself, and we didn't know what had happened to you. The constable checked the house and saw the food left out—but wouldn't let us stay to clean it up—we've been so worried." Holding a cloth-covered basket aside, Lettie Banks wrapped Belinda in a fierce hug, and Belinda remembered something she often forgot in the gray: she wasn't completely without friends here, even if they weren't her age or the sisters she wanted to love her.

Lettie released her and stepped back to take in Belinda's appearance and overall look of health. She finished her inspection with a satisfied nod and handed off the basket to her. The aroma of freshly baked bread soothed Belinda's soul. "I thought you might like something fresh until you have time to settle in."

"I—" Belinda glanced from the basket to the valise. "Thank you." She opened her mouth as if to say something else, then shut it.

With a curious glance at her, Lettie took the basket back

and led the way to the kitchen, Belinda following. Taking over as hostess, Lettie saw to the teapot while Belinda served them bread and jam.

"You just rest yourself there and talk now, young miss," Lettie said after Belinda finally settled at the table, bread and jam spread out before her. "Who is this Lady Violetta that your letter mentioned you've been working for? And why did your father's note to us not mention your disappearance? We wrote to him as soon as we realized you were missing. *He* could have at least told us you were safe, even if you didn't."

Belinda bit down on her piece of bread harder than intended, partly in shame and partly in irritation. *Meddling enchantress.* Lady Violetta had fixed things with her father not getting word about her disappearance but not fixed her disappearance by leaving a note on her door for Lettie and Winthrop to find. Too sensible a solution for her, apparently.

Well, at least her father hadn't worried.

How would he feel about a longer separation?

When she looked up at the tea kettle's whistle, she found Lettie watching her with that curious expression again. Lettie saw to the stove, then brought the kettle over.

"My father's gone for another three weeks. I'm thinking of going back," Belinda blurted, looking more at her hands than at Lettie. "Either way, I need to let Be—my escort know my decision. He's waiting in the forest."

A knowing expression overtook the curiosity in Lettie's gaze as she settled into the chair across from Belinda. Her eyes twinkled with motherly affection and mischief. "And is this escort nice, my dear?"

Belinda's cheeks flamed. "Yes. Very, but—"

Switching to motherly mentor, Lettie narrowed her eyes. "Thoroughly respectable? Honorable? Kind? A man of faith? A man of integrity?"

"Yes to all," Belinda couldn't help but answer with pride, "but—"

Lettie leaned back in her chair. "Then let him wait. See how he takes it, just to be sure."

A laugh escaped Belinda. "But what would that say about me?"

Lettie shrugged, her eyes twinkling as she snagged a piece of bread. "Just don't make a habit of it."

Belinda grinned, despite the war in her mind. "What news while I was away?"

"Well, my dear," Lettie answered in a conspirator's whisper as she leaned forward, "I'm afraid you missed all the drama—all who got sick got well again, all who were engaged got married." She shook her head in mock disappointment.

"What a pity," Belinda said, biting back a smile.

"Yes, isn't it? And then—" She and Belinda both groaned at a pounding on the front door.

"Lindie pie! I know you're home." Gaspard's shout was loud enough to reach the far reaches of the house at the end of the lane.

"He's been off hunting a great deal lately," Lettie said with a sympathetic look at Belinda, "leaving the shop to his apprentice. I was hoping for your sake he'd be gone for a while longer. I'd suggest reasoning with him, but we both know how useful that is." She rose and brushed off her skirt. "I can give you five minutes—if you promise to let me know you're safe and tell me more about this exceptional young man."

Belinda glanced between Lettie, the direction of the rattling front door, and her hand clinging to her yellow shawl, then leapt up and embraced her friend. "I'll write." She grabbed her valise and darted out the back door as Lettie opened the front.

Belinda crept through the yard but began to run as soon

as she left the village. Not far into the forest, she collapsed against a gnarled mulberry to catch her breath. After reminding herself to get more exercise while at the castle, she switched the valise from one hand to the other and marched on.

Her mouth, she soon discovered, was determined to curve, either in a smile or a frown, but mostly satisfying itself with a smile.

It was still smiling as she approached the tree with the hollow.

"Beast, my father's not returning for three weeks. I've—"

There was no Beast in sight, and he was too large for the hollow. She stifled the gray thought that he'd returned to the castle without her and trudged on. He was probably walking around to stretch his legs after waiting for so long.

"Beast?" she called, peering through the bushes and trees to her left.

The prick of a dagger against her spine drew her attention back to the path. Belinda slowly raised her hands, praying Beast had the good sense to stay well away.

"Really, Gaspard, this isn't—"

"Is Beast running from you too now, Miss Lambton?" asked a saccharine voice. "How tragic." The blade slid along Belinda's ribcage as Lucrezia moved to her side, in view.

"Never from *me*," Belinda shot, struggling to stifle both a start and a tremor of fear. What did the woman think she could accomplish by waylaying and threatening her?

The blade dug a little deeper, but Belinda refused to squirm. She was no shrinking violet, and the sooner Lucrezia realized it, the better. Surprisingly, that smile threatened to curve her lips again. She knew a few disarming tricks. She might get to bloody Lucrezia's nose after all. And even Beast couldn't say it wasn't justified.

"Stop it, Lucrezia." Robert and a half-dozen soldiers

wearing the Duke of Marblue's livery stepped from the forest, from behind bushes and trees that shouldn't have hidden them so well.

Her heart, like her hopes, dropped to the trampled leaves. When this was over, she was going to suggest—very strongly—on an investigation of the Guild of Practicing Enchanters. Someone was helping Lucrezia, and it wasn't, any longer, Lady Violetta. Even *she* wasn't so foolish or malicious.

"Ordering me around is bad enough. Leave the girl alone."

"She's not worth your concern, Robert." With a contemptuous huff, Lucrezia sheathed the dagger as Robert took his stand beside Belinda.

Belinda gave him a commiserating look as she crossed her arms in front of her and gave Lucrezia a defiant smile.

He touched her lightly on the arm and turned to the duke's daughter, a dangerous fire in his eyes. "This has gone too far. I'm going to tell my uncle—"

"Go into the woods until I call for you, Robert." Lucrezia waved dismissively to the trees on her right, her other hand rubbing her golden locket as if in thoughtless habit.

Robert choked on his words and tugged his ear. Gritting his teeth, he dragged his arm to his side. "Lucrezia—"

"Go, Robert. Quietly."

Hatred simmering in his eyes, hand tugging his ear, Robert walked to the forest, stiffly, like a puppet on a string.

"What do you want?" Belinda balled her fists, never wishing so strongly in her life that daggers really could be shot from eyes. She knew the perfect target.

"Playing dumb comes naturally to you, doesn't it?"

Belinda smiled sweetly and widened her eyes. "Whatever do you mean, Lucrezia dear?"

Lucrezia tapped her jeweled fingers on her arm, her eyes narrowing dangerously. She had a ring for every finger and occasion, except for a marriage, Belinda noted with great satisfaction.

"Where's Beast?" Lucrezia's short tone was reminiscent of a cannon whose fuse was not overlong.

Belinda made a show of glancing around. "Not where I left him."

She felt the imprint of those rings on her cheek.

"Tie her up," Lucrezia ordered. She wiped her hand on her handkerchief as she backed away.

The soldiers complied with an adeptness indicating no mean amount of experience. Belinda would also report that.

After she found a way to unbind her hands and feet, of course. But at least the gag choking her kept the leaves and dirt from the hard ground out of her mouth. How considerate of Lucrezia. She'd have to repay the favor sometime.

Belinda's heart stilled. What if the next time she saw her, the woman was wife to an unwilling Beast? Such a gray fate for him. And all because of her. A stab of a different kind pierced her chest. Belinda bit back an angry cry and focused on her defiance, the red and the blue, the yellow—a righteous anger with a touch of vengeance, the color of something very valuable, and hope. They could fight the pale gray of defeat and the thunderous gray of fear.

Lucrezia drew a thin wooden whistle from inside her cloak and trilled a bird-like call that impressed Belinda despite herself. Even villains had talents other than pure villainy, she conceded. After putting away the whistle, Lucrezia called Robert back.

He sputtered in anger after nearly tripping over Belinda as he marched toward Lucrezia. He jumped back, hollering, "What the blazes are you thinking, tying her up?" Quickly regaining his footing and some of his composure, he began to kneel beside Belinda, but the guards blocked him.

"That's not a girl, Robert."

"But it is," he insisted, pushing one guard aside. The soldier stood down at a flick of Lucrezia's wrist.

"It's not a girl, Robert."

"Then what the blazes is it?" he roared. He tugged at his ear, helplessly. His eyes begged Belinda for something, but what could she do for him? She tried stretching her legs out to kick Lucrezia but was reminded of the length of rope connecting her bound hands to her bound feet. "But it's got to be ..." he said more quietly.

Sighing, Lucrezia waved at Belinda. "If an enchantress can turn your cousin into a beast, cannot one turn an animal into a dumb human? It's another of her tricks to keep us from uncursing him. You must trust me, Robert. I want him uncursed as much as you do, for the kingdom."

He opened his mouth but tugged his ear. "Then what is it really?" He watched Belinda, his alert expression fading in and out to glassy.

"A skunk," Lucrezia said drily.

Belinda mouthed her name as she focused on Robert's blue eyes. *Fight it, Robert. Fight it.*

Face tight, as if some battle were going on inside, Robert finally shook his head. "I still say it's Miss Lambton, and you shouldn't treat her like that."

Lucrezia's chest rose and fell with a heavy sigh. "Robert, you try my patience. I can't believe that idiot enchantress's spell gave me you instead of—" She stopped and eyed Belinda, a knowing smile on her face. "At least you're finally going to be useful to me." She drew a slender knife from the sheath hanging from her belt and then took a black vial from her handbag. "I hadn't wanted to do this, but I don't have much time. Uncover her mouth."

The guard roughly uncovered Belinda's mouth as Robert stepped forward, his hand on his sword hilt.

"I won't let you harm her."

Lucrezia tipped the vial, letting a single, bloodred drop spatter onto the blade and run down the metal to the silver guard. She turned to him, her voice as saccharine as her smile. "Oh, Robert, this isn't for *her*." Her skirts brushed Belinda's feet as she swept forward and buried the blade in Robert's side.

"No!" Belinda screamed. Two guards pinned her to the ground as she struggled to get her feet underneath her. "Robert!"

He lurched back, lips bound against a cry. Lucrezia slid the blade out and drew back again.

"Stop it! Please!"

Robert flinched at Belinda's scream but no one else paid her any mind. He grabbed Lucrezia's wrist, stopping the blade just short of his stomach. The soldiers made no move against him, just watched as the daughter of a duke and a king's guard strained for control of a bloodied knife.

Perhaps because they knew they wouldn't have to inter-fere. Robert's face was deathly pale and slightly green, his soldier's arm trembling.

"Stop it!" Belinda cried again. The guard's booted foot pressed against her shoulder, pushing her side into the dirt.

Lucrezia's lips curved into a smug smile. The stained blade's tip teased the fabric shielding Robert's other side. "Say it again, Belinda," she said sweetly. "*Beg* for him."

His jaw clenched, Robert locked gazes with Belinda and shook his head, only able to risk that distraction, that diver-gence of his strength.

"Please, stop," Belinda said softly. She wouldn't *not* cower if it helped him. "Let him be."

"Scream it." The blade pricked Robert's stomach.

Not caring about pride or dignity, and saving all her loathing for another time, Belinda filled her lungs and opened her mouth. But the scream caught in her throat.

Beast was near enough to hear her. Robert knew it. That's why he wouldn't scream for himself or have her scream for him.

Belinda went cold, her throat closing up on its own. What had she done? She locked gazes with Lucrezia, and Lucrezia smiled.

"Yes, by one king's grandson or the other, I'll get my crown. I'll have a son who'll be king. And you've just helped me."

Robert swayed as tremors swept over him. Lucrezia stepped back. He collapsed, unconscious, to the blood-splattered ground.

The rustling of leaves and limbs, the trampling of many feet sounded from deeper in the forest. A hound bayed. A whoosh of air warned of a dart or arrow. A heavy thump brought it all to silence.

A second thin rush of air preceded a sharp pain in Belinda's back and darkness.

CHAPTER 15

Belinda woke with a squint and a flinch, and the realization that water was dripping down her face while a rag was clumsily wiping it off. She risked opening one eye and found Gaspard's face too close for comfort. Though uncertain why he was waking her up when Beast almost invariably did that after she dreamed, she instinctively tried to lean back and found she couldn't. Why not? She'd always woken mobile before. She *had* just been dreaming, right? Lucrezia had been there and—

She gasped, horror twisting her already nauseated stomach. A few mental shakes of her head and her mind cleared enough for her to remember Lucrezia and Robert and Beast, and to realize her hands were tied in front of her and she was sitting propped up against a tree deep in the forest. Gaspard's pack of hounds lounged a few feet away, judging by the pungent odor of sweaty dog and the trampling of leaves. Ready to catch her should she try to run?

Everything went gray and red.

"You'll never get away with this, you know."

Her heart lurched at the familiar voice. He didn't belong in this mess!

Gaspard turned to scowl at Winthrop Banks, her pastor, her friend, who sounded more annoyed than fearful. Belinda envied him. The rag left her face. Without the pressure of Gaspard's hand to hold it up, Belinda's head lolled to the side, letting her steal a glimpse of the tall, trim Winthrop. He was standing a half-dozen feet away, his bound hands in front of him, clasping a Bible. He matched Gaspard's glower. Tucked against his side more by habit than by intimidation, Lettie held a stationery kit in her bound hands. A few paces behind them, sitting sleepily in the back of a cart, with blankets bunched around them, were Gaspard's great-aunt and great-uncle. With the temperaments of cats, sometimes sweet and sometimes snappish, the wizened couple hadn't known what was going on for the past three years.

"I should say not," Lettie agreed. She caught Belinda's eye, spied that she was awake, and winked at her. Belinda's heart knotted at the gesture meant to encourage her. Knowing Lettie, the woman probably assumed Belinda's "escort" would come along any minute to save them. Or that Gaspard wouldn't truly hurt them.

Refusing to consider the futility of hoping for the former, Belinda absorbed some of the woman's spirit and tried to infuse it into her weak muscles.

Her thoughts strayed to worry over Beast and Robert, but she quickly roped them into something useful and narrowed her eyes at the back of Gaspard's head. What she wouldn't give for a poisoned dagger of her own. Two of them.

Or three of them.

Three of what? Belinda blinked and struggled to retain that momentary focus. She hated sleeping darts.

Gaspard grunted as he turned back to Belinda. "I'll get away with it. She'll see that I do. Her ladyship's word would slaughter yours afore the magistrates." He tossed the rag away as he noted Belinda's open eyes.

"Remind me to pray for the reformation of court proceedings, my dear," Winthrop said sardonically. "They sound rather more violent than I supposed them to be."

"This will go to the king," Belinda ground out, using the lingering feel of cotton in her mouth to round up her stray thoughts and focus that slight spinning of the world.

Standing her up, Gaspard rolled his eyes. "A wife can't testify against her husband."

"I'm not—"

"You will be!" Gaspard's shout cleared away the lingering effects of the sleeping dart, though she still needed his hand on her shoulder to stay upright.

Her skin burning under his touch, she let herself fall back against the tree as support. "What did you do to Beast?"

Gaspard bared his teeth in a feral grin that sickened her. What had become of her onetime friend? "Only sent him where he belongs: to the tower to rot for attempted murder and kidnapping."

"What!"

After a smirk at her, Gaspard called over his shoulder, "Ready to start the wedding, Banks?" He turned back to Belinda and leaned close. "Congratulate me, bride," he whispered. "I helped the daughter of the king's greatest ally capture the cursed blackguard who'd tried to assassinate the king and the prince three years ago. And was paid handsomely for it."

Sick and stunned beyond words, Belinda could only stare at him and turn her face away as he leaned in to kiss her. He brushed her cheek with a kiss, then spun around to the pastor.

Winthrop's gaze threatened hellfire as his knuckles whitened around his Bible.

"The wedding, Banks?" Gaspard's pistol turned the question into an order. By accident or design, he kept it aimed in Lettie's direction.

With a look around, at the hounds and the woods and Lettie, Winthrop rolled his shoulders, as if dropping his fury to cool his mind, and then began, very, very slowly.

Beast imprisoned. Robert stabbed and poisoned. Gaspard threatening her friends to force a marriage, even dragging his frail great-aunt and great-uncle into the woods to act as witnesses. It was too much. Belinda's focus threatened to sink within herself, to pretend this wasn't happening, that nothing she remembered of the day had happened.

But that was the gray, and she had to fight it. Beast and Robert depended on it. She *would* help them. She latched onto Winthrop's proud, calm voice, wanting to steal that calmness to disperse the gray and cool the red into something useful.

As her husband spoke, Lettie looked everywhere but at Belinda. At Gaspard, she aimed a warrior's fierceness. To the forest surrounding them, she applied the lookout's trade, expectation in her face but no light of discovery. Did she expect someone?

Winthrop paused, his sharp gaze leaping from Belinda to his wife to the forest and back. He gave Lettie a curious glance, and she gave him a shrug.

"Go on," Gaspard prodded, reinforcing the command with the motion of his pistol.

With the glare he generally reserved for the editorials, Winthrop directed his gaze and words to Gaspard. "By the power vested in me, I declare you man and woman."

Tightening his grip on her shoulder, Gaspard leaned down while pulling Belinda toward him. She steeled herself to bite him and likely get slapped for it.

"Wait!" Winthrop ordered. "It's not time for that yet."

"Yes, it is," Gaspard protested, but he straightened. "I've been to a wedding before."

Belinda let out her breath and relaxed against the tree. He'd free her hands eventually, and then she'd be ready for him.

"Doubtless, you have, and, doubtless," Winthrop said, drawing himself up and continuing with a snooty tone, "it wasn't so rushed as this. You need to sign the certificate first." He flipped open the Bible's cover and awkwardly withdrew a folded sheet of paper. He held it out.

Sighing like a martyr, Gaspard holstered his pistol and took the sheet from Winthrop. He reached for the Bible as a solid surface to sign on, but Winthrop drew it back.

Holding the book above his head, Winthrop said, petulantly, "Sign it on the tree. I don't want the ink bleeding onto my Bible. This is the one I use for ceremonies."

Gaspard rolled his eyes but took the quill from Lettie and waited as Winthrop gently prodded Belinda from the support of the tree trunk to one of its low limbs. With a discreet wink, he scooted between her and the trunk. Lettie stood across from her. He waved Gaspard toward the makeshift writing desk.

While Belinda swayed and struggled to convince her muscles that they wanted to keep her upright, Gaspard rolled his eyes again as he betook himself and the paper to the indicated spot and leaned against the tree. "Just here?" he mockingly asked Winthrop as he rested the paper against the bark.

"Perfect."

Muttering something under his breath, Gaspard turned back to the paper and began to sign his name.

Winthrop's lips quirked into a smile just before his Bible rammed into the back of Gaspard's head, cracking Gaspard's forehead against the hard white oak. Lettie snagged Gaspard's pistol with her bound hands and rapped him on the head with it for good measure as her husband yanked him down to her level.

Gaspard went limp, and Winthrop caught him under one arm as Lettie tossed the pistol into the leaves, then grabbed Gaspard's other arm.

"Lettie, my dear, you truly are a companion for all times."

Huffing under Gaspard's weight, Lettie grinned over his head to her husband. "For better or for worse, my love."

He nodded in agreement, then gave Belinda a sideways glance as they lowered the unconscious Gaspard to the ground. "Yes, and remind me to include 'in matchmaking and in mayhem' should we ever renew our vows." He huffed as he released Gaspard's arm. "That man is all muscle." He huffed again, then straightened his shoulders, his tone turning formal as he began pilfering through Gaspard's pockets for a knife. "If any know of an impediment to the union of this man and this woman, speak now or forever hold your peace."

Belinda opened her mouth to respond, but he cut her off. "Yes, I personally can think of several, not the least of which is kidnapping the intended bride—and the pastor's wife."

When he ended his narrow-eyed glare at Gaspard, his brown eyes lit on Belinda, and his attempt at mock solemnness gave way to a twinkle. He sat back on his heels, a knife in his hand. "I'm sorry, Miss Lambton, but there will be no wedding today."

"After I spent so much on the dress and flowers and food!" she said, the words rough in her dry throat. "And invited so many people. It's humiliating. Please, *don't* reconsider."

He chuckled and carefully freed Lettie's wrists, then gave her the knife to use against their bonds. Lettie cut Belinda's, then his.

"I'm disappointed in this young man Lettie assured me would rescue us all," he said as Lettie gave him back the knife. He eyed Gaspard, then tucked the knife away in his own pocket before sifting through the bushes for the pistol and doing likewise with it. "I'm afraid I had to take the honor from him. What do you think became of him?"

"Gaspard, a sleeping dart, and the daughter of the Duke of Marblue," Belinda growled as she rubbed her free wrists. Shaking off the red and gray, she dared a step and found her legs bending but not giving completely. "I can't explain right now. I have to get help. I think he's been imprisoned in the tower."

Lettie blanched. "There was a commotion in the town going toward the old keep before Gaspard forced us out here. I thought at the time it'd have to be the king or a real prisoner to cause such a racket. But if the Duke of Marblue is involved—"

Wincing at Lettie's choice of comparison, Belinda laid a hand on Lettie's arm and stood on tiptoe to kiss Winthrop's cheek. "Then nothing good will come of it. Thanks, you two. I'm going to get help. Whatever you hear about a beast or a cursed man in the dungeon, he's innocent. Remember that."

"The warden's not exactly a loyal flock member, but I can try talking to him and at least make sure the prisoner is well taken care of," Winthrop offered, catching her hand as she turned away.

"Please do, but be careful if you see any of the Duke of Marblue's men."

"What—"

Tugging her hand free, Belinda prayed the way to the castle would still be open to her. The day was dimming already. "I have to go! I love you both!"

"What help will she find in the forest?" Winthrop asked as Belinda darted away.

CHAPTER 16

The darkening clouds swirled under the glass floor of the Observation Room as Lyndon paced and Belinda sat at the desk, clasping the mirror, watching Beast sleep chained to a stone wall.

"We're the only two who can leave the castle grounds," Lyndon protested. "I *have* to go to the tower, and *you* must ride for the king. I bear his livery. They'll listen to me, at least until you can get King Patrick there."

Once again, Belinda shook her head and called out, "Lady Violetta! Come! Please, come!" She looked up through the glass roof, as if the enchantress lived in the sky rather than some fashionable house in town. But looking up reminded her to pray as well.

Only Lyndon's exasperated huff came in reply. Did the enchantress only answer when Belinda was in front of her mirror holding a hairbrush?

Refusing to let her shoulders droop, Belinda turned back to Lyndon. "The Duke of Marblue's men won't respect you. At the very least they'll lock you up as an accomplice."

Lyndon's hand cut through the air in a gesture of exasperation. "I hope the king hangs them for this. As to me being in danger, Lucrezia knows both of us. You won't be safe either. We need to go anyway—me to the tower and you to the king —and we must leave now." He scooped up the mirror and tucked his hand under Belinda's elbow to help her up. "Please, Belinda." The desperation in his eyes tore at her already fragile heart.

"Please, wait just a moment more," she pleaded, rising anyway. "We'd be too slow going for the king without—" A burst of rainbow-colored light in the center of the room reflected off the glass walls with blinding brilliance before coalescing into a violet cloud floating beyond the desk. The cloud sank to the floor, slowly unveiling Lady Violetta. She shifted ever so slightly as she stood, letting the light sparkle off a shimmering violet gown. The fabric and jewel creation was tame by Lady Violetta's standards, but still wide enough to fill a carriage by itself.

She nodded regally at Lyndon and smiled at Belinda. "I really hope you have good news, my dear. Not to scold," she said in a mildly censoring tone, the kind one would use on a favorite pooch who just destroyed a favorite wand, "but I was in the middle of a most engaging dinner party, and leaving guests is so rude. I was getting their opinion on my new creation—I whipped it up with you in mind in case, you know —What a brilliant room! Did I do this?" Clapping her hands in glee, Lady Violetta began strolling the length of the glass thorn-shaped room.

Snatching the mirror from the stunned Lyndon, Belinda snagged Lady Violetta's voluminous skirt before she could get too far away. "You've got to help! She's caught him and impris- oned him."

Lady Violetta froze mid-tweak of her gown and glanced at the mirror Belinda held in front of her. Her violet eyes went pale before darkening to a deep, dangerous amethyst.

"Oh no, she doesn't." Drawing herself up, she snapped her fingers. Black mist swirled about her feet, and her wand lengthened to a scepter. Her hair lost its shimmer but gained a tiara of black diamonds. Her gown slimmed to an austere robe of black with a silver belt of diamonds and bloodred rubies. Eyes flashing, she tapped the scepter against the floor. The swirling black mist vanished. "No one's spoiling my curse."

Mouth agape, Belinda stepped back, very carefully. Had she called forth some sort of mistress of evil?

Brushing past Belinda to the desk, Lady Violetta pushed up her sleeves and sat. She pulled a piece of stationery from the desk to her, and a violet-feathered quill drawn from somewhere in the ether appeared. She looked up at Belinda, quill poised, eyes intent. "Now, what are we going to do?"

Belinda's knees gave way. She grabbed the edge of the desk as Lyndon caught her by the arm. "Um ..."

"Um ..." Lady Violetta repeated, leaning over the paper as she began to write. "Um ... Umbrage?" She glanced up at Belinda. "Yes, I take great offense at this matter too, as will the king."

"Um ... that's not ... I meant ..."

"Umbrella!" Lady Violetta supplied cheerfully. "Though I'm not sure how useful it would be. It's not raining at the moment, though"—she looked through the floor—"it might be soon. Such forethought you have. And I could put a spell on it! *That* would be useful."

"No ... I ..." Movement in the mirror caught Belinda's attention. Beast shifted in his sleep, wincing as if in pain. It twisted something inside her, tugging all her stray thoughts, fears, and plans back into place. She pressed her hand to her heart, as if doing so could somehow hold all those things there, as if they could hold her heart together long enough to rescue Beast. "I need you to send Lyndon to King Patrick, then both to the tower in my village," she blurted. "Preferably with a unit of guards."

Lady Violetta blinked, then set down her quill in a suddenly appearing gold inkwell. She exhaled a delicate sigh. "My job would be so much easier if everyone knew the rules and limitations of magic. I can't, I'm afraid, magically vaporize, transport, and un-vaporize more than one person to one place. No moving of armies, for certain." She lifted her shoulders in a slight shrug. "Rules. Not to mention that maintaining this curse for three years has been draining." She paused, seemingly seeking sympathy, then added before Belinda or Lyndon could speak, "And I should probably mention that I can't do anything directly. Nothing to prevent Lucrezia from forcing him to propose."

A bolt of gray went through Belinda's heart. Blast gray! "Then send Lyndon. That would cut half the time to get the king to the tower. If you could help me get in to Beast"—Lady Violetta's nodding and retrieval of her quill encouraged Belinda to continue with what seemed hopeless —"maybe we can sneak him out as a ... flower in my hair or something."

The quill drooped. "I'm afraid you can't do a second transformation spell on someone. Only one spell at a time. The spells might get mixed up, and who knows what the end result would be."

Belinda blanched. "Oh."

"Yes, but back to"—the quill began writing on its own as Lady Violetta spoke—"*get Belinda into the cell with Beast* idea. I like that one. *Very* promising." Her smile was decidedly sly, but Belinda didn't have time to consider it.

"You can do that?" she asked in surprise.

Lady Violetta cocked an eyebrow. "Of course—oh." She flicked her hand in Lyndon's direction, and he vanished with a startled cry. The quill made a check mark on the cream-colored parchment. "Part One: Message to King Patrick. *Check.* Part Two ..."

⚜

BELINDA WAS GOING to make a grand entrance. At least that's what Lady Violetta had assured her. The stone of the tower keep was cold under Belinda's fingers, damp and slimy with growth of some foul sort. How was she going to get through that rock? Marigold nudged her shoulder, and Belinda rubbed her muzzle in return, whispering "Stay," into her twitching ear.

A silencing spell had helped get them, along with the largest horse in the stable, into the village and hidden beside the tower in a little-used alleyway. A dark, hooded cloak and a uniform matching the Duke of Marblue's guards kept them from being questioned by any who saw them. It was one of three outfits Lady Violetta had included in Belinda's arsenal. She'd not divulged the other two, which would magically appear when called on. Belinda would have to trust that the enchantress's surprisingly practical choice of the first continued to the rest.

And then there was the rose ...

Belinda folded back the flap of her satchel and blinked against the rosy glow radiating from it. From an open box, she pulled a heavy golden vase the height of her hand. A sad smile twisted her lips as she held the vase up to admire it. It wasn't a delicate thing she feared breaking. It had a look of strength and solidness about its masculine design. Polished gold, the emblem of the kingdom engraved into it, set with sapphires, rubies, emeralds, and diamonds. It was beautiful and strong. Like its owner.

An idea teased her mind and her eyes when she stared too long at it: it was wrought of a crown.

A rose, thorned and glowing, rested against the vase's lip. The glow wasn't the soft pink of a sunrise or the dusty rose of a sunset. It was the same deep crimson hue as the bloodred petals clinging to the rose hip, limp and sparse. It was an aging rose for an aging curse. *Why, Beast? Is danger a game for you?* She brushed a finger gently over a drooping petal. It was soft as fur on one touch, silken as a young rose on the next.

The rose is the sign and focus of Beast's curse, Lady Violetta had said. *It cannot be kept apart from him. Don't worry. You can't cause a petal to drop; nor can he deliberately pluck them off. Curses have rules.*

Belinda clenched her jaw. Curse curses and their rules. At least the ones Lucrezia took advantage of. *But uncurse stubborn beasts who won't give them up,* she added in prayer. She opened her left palm and balanced the vase out before her. Calling up an image of Beast, with teasing merriment in his eyes as they raced together, Belinda held the rose in front of her. "Take me, please," she said, and walked into the impenetrable tower wall.

A crimson glow exploded around her. Vine-like strands of gold flared and twisted through the blaze, shooting out and retreating, brushing against the wall and the alley floor, reaching under her hood to tickle through her hair, darting forward to some unknown target and then flying back to her chest to settle against her heart and tug her along. She jerked back at the contact, then eased forward, the tension of her shoulders giving way to the warmth of the golden flare thrumming against her heart with a pulse of its own.

The wall vanished, as did the alley behind her. The golden thread drew her along, twining through the tower's secret ways, paths found only by magic and sly, creeping creatures. Through the crimson haze of light and flashes of gold, she could just make out the lines of stones stacked and joined together, the dark blotches of spiders on gossamer webs, the gray, scurrying forms of mice and lizards.

Stone and web and creatures all gave way to let her pass. No web caught her hair nor rough rock her fingers.

Then her feet felt the push back of solid stone beneath, a silent refusal to give way for her. Cool, musty air assaulted her face. Lowering the rose, she looked about her and instantly stiffened.

She was a small figure in a cavernous room, perched high on a rail-less stair whose apparent purpose was access to the cage, wrought of iron bands and sized to fit a man, hanging above her. Empty racks lined the walls where weapons and instruments of cruelty once hung. A few broken remnants of larger machines sat about the room. A trapdoor in the floor, nearer the wall than the center of the room, marked the exit of the criminals and traitors who'd entered. Tightening her grip on the vase as if it could shield her from the ghosts of the past conjuring violent images in her mind, she forced her eyes away. Higher up, to her left, at the solitary break in the stone wall, was a barred window, perhaps as wide as Belinda's shoulders. Certainly not Beast's.

"To him," she whispered. Her heart jumped to her throat. The stone beneath her feet gave way. The bloodred glow enveloped her again, and she fell as much as walked, following the golden tendrils to the black heart of the tower.

Stone once again refused to let her pass. Black and red blended. The yellow and orange of a flame danced with them, and then the red glow fled back to her, darkness following. But darkness couldn't conquer the yellow and orange.

Across the room—a dungeon cell—light from a small window high in a heavy wooden door reinforced with iron bands cast shadows on the wall to play with those from the twin torches flickering yellow and orange on the walls flanking the door. Shadows and light both outlined a familiar form chained, standing, to the wall. His head hung forward as if in sleep. Dark flakes of dried blood stained his cuffs. Dirt and grass smudged his velvet jacket.

The rose's glow dwindled to a blush of the air around it, and the golden threads retreated to the vase, except the one that kept its coiling path to Beast's chest, connecting him with the rose and her. The golden thread burst loose from Beast with a fiery jolt that Belinda felt in her own chest. It vanished into the vase with a golden spark, and Beast's head snapped up.

"Beast!" With the silencing spell still in effect, she could only be heard if she wished it. And she wished it now. She pulled back her hood.

He straightened as if forgetting his chains, that hideous, toothy grin breaking across his face. "Belinda! What—" He clamped his mouth shut, his gaze jerking to the door opposite him. His look of horror was almost comical. He was chained to a wall, yet concerned for her.

"Don't look so alarmed. I'm no ghost," she tried to tease as she picked her way over rotting straw strewn across worn stone. But her attempt fell flat. She didn't have the heart for it with him chained like a criminal. Well, she was here to change that. Making her spine as stiff as a book's, she forced a confident tone. "I have a silencing spell. I'm only heard by those I wish to talk with, and so long as I want, they're only heard by me."

She left the corner's shadows, the rose still held out in front of her. The joy faded from Beast's face as his gaze fell on the rose and rested there, his expression shifting from shock to unreadable.

Liar. Traitor. Spy for the enchantress. Illiterate villager trickster.

The accusations swarming her mind pierced her like a rose's thorns. Guilt knotting off her words, Belinda slipped the rose back into her satchel and covered it. As she did, a single petal loosened and floated to rest on her boots. It shifted to a warning tuft of chestnut fur, then vanished.

Belinda sucked in her breath and looked with horror to Beast, but he didn't seem surprised. *He knows exactly when each petal will fall. He knows exactly how long he has.* He meant to keep his curse until the last moment. Stubborn fool.

She might think him a fool, but what did he think of her?

"The rose was the only way to reach you," Belinda said hastily, crossing the straw-dusted floor between them. *But it isn't a way to get out.* "I didn't know Lady Violetta before I came to the castle. I swear it, Beast. I didn't lie to you."

He watched her as she approached and hesitantly examined his shackles, yet didn't respond. She pulled a ring of old rusted keys from her satchel. *Say something, Beast. Anything.*

She tried a key in the lock, then another, neither turning it. "She just showed up that first afternoon and nearly scared me out of my wits," she said, comparing the tip of the next key to the lock's opening.

A chuckle rumbled softly in Beast's chest, plugging the holes his silence and her guilt had made in her own.

Gathering her pluck, she smiled archly. "She asked me to help her out with a curse on a rather stubborn, anonymous individual." Her smile fell. "I guess I didn't have a right to interfere, but she said it was for the good of the kingdom and my father, so I told her I would try." She hurried on, finally daring to meet his eye for a brief second as she fit the last key into the lock. "I can't break the curse, but he can ... and I wish he would, before it's too late." *I don't ask you to do it for me. I know I don't have that right, but please, you've kept it long enough.*

A sad smile barely curved Beast's lips in acknowledgement. "I'm glad you're okay, Belinda," he said at last, his voice thick. "When I heard you screaming earlier, I thought ..." He shuddered.

Stretching up, she slid her hand into his, startling him

before he closed his hand around hers. "I wasn't screaming for myself."

He bowed his head. "She was telling the truth then? About Robert being hurt?"

"Yes ... It's partly my fault. He was trying to protect me— You've talked with her?" An arrow, tipped with gray but thatched with red, pierced her. She clutched at the red. *If noble Beast thought he had to marry that woman because of some stupid curse's forced proposal, she'd ... she'd knock some sense into him!* She yanked her hand back to her chest, keys clanking as she put away the useless collection.

A hint of a smile flashed across Beast's face. "I pretended to be unconscious when Lucrezia came in to gloat. She didn't buy it but said her piece and warned she'd be back tomorrow for my answer." The unexpected lightness to his voice quickly faded to seriousness, and Belinda's hands slowed to a more sure than reckless pace as she searched the recesses of her satchel.

"Has he a chance?" Beast asked, his whole heart seeming to be in the question. "Robert's like my brother, and it's my fault. Not yours."

Her hand paused its search, considering both the vial beneath her fingers and the question. "I'm no physician," she said slowly, releasing the vial and withdrawing her hand, "but I think, poison reversed, the wound could go either way." She balled her fist around the satchel's leather strap. "I think that was the intent." Lucrezia liked to hold on to all her cards.

Beast nodded, but then straightened, rattling the chains, reminding Belinda to include them in her silencing spell. "Do you have any angry skunks or rabid raccoons up your sleeve, Miss Lambton?"

"I did promise I would earn my keep." Forcing down the ever-present gray, she called up her best cheeky grin and pulled a short, round jar from the satchel and unscrewed its lid. "No animals this time, I'm sorry to confess, *but* I have something else." She dipped two fingers into the thick, greasy potion filling the jar and began rubbing it around his left palm and wrist, careful not to get any on the shackles.

Beast watched, incredulous. "No amount of grease is going to get my thick paws out of these chains."

"This isn't grease. It's a mild, temporary shrinking potion." And it smelled of strawberries, which she found rather unnerving.

Beast's gaze darted from the jar to his wrists, his eyes widening. "A ... what! Belinda, if you got that from the enchantress I think you got that from, I don't want it." The rusty iron chains clanged as he tried to shift his wrist away from Belinda's potion-lathered hands.

"Don't be silly," she said, grabbing for his paw. "You don't want to stay here, do you?"

Beast opened his mouth but then shut it. Belinda captured his wrist without trouble and recommenced application.

"I hope you know that stuff is not comfortable in fur," he groused as she moved around him to his other wrist.

"Then get rid of your fur."

Beast's gaze bored into her, then darted away.

That's right. Think on it. She dabbed her fingers into the potion and gently touched the fur of his wrist, her heart twisting as she rubbed over dried blood and torn flesh. He flinched ever so slightly but didn't complain. "Big baby," she teased.

He cocked an eyebrow at her, then assumed an offended tilt to his chin. "You're lucky I'm sweet-natured. Any other beast would eat you for this."

"You terrify me."

"So I've noticed."

She laughed.

"I'd like to terrify Gaspard," he added with a growl a moment later. "You wouldn't try to distract me this time, I trust?"

"I imagine you'd have to fight the constable for him, but I wouldn't object." She gave the wild fur of his wrist a smoothing pat, then held her own hands up in front of her. They looked ... oddly small. Flexing her fingers, she brought her hands closer, wrinkled her nose at the strawberry-ish odor, and held her hands out again. Definitely smaller.

It *worked*. It actually worked!

Stifling a giggle at her ridiculous appendages, she returned the jar to her satchel and wiped her palms on her cloak. She wrapped both hands around Beast's forearm. "Try to work your paw—sorry, I know you prefer *hand*—down through the shackle while I tug."

His arm muscles stiffened under her fingers. "The shackles aren't going to suddenly shrink when the potion on my hands hits them, are they? Because then I'll be stuck, and the potion on my wrists will wear out before the potion on the shackles."

"Oh ... um ... We'll just hurry. On my mark: *Austen ... Brönte ... Shakespeare!*"

She tugged, he squeezed, his hand slipped out, she tumbled back. His body went limp and fell away toward the support of his bound hand. She grabbed for his jacket as his other hand slid free under his weight. He fell back against the wall, Belinda toppling with him. Beast grabbed her round the waist, and they landed on the floor, with a thump and a poof of dust and straw, Belinda safely in Beast's lap.

"Why, Miss Lambton," Beast said, grinning at her without the slightest move to release her, rather tightening his hold about her waist. "I didn't think you were the type to throw yourself at eligible bachelors."

The ghastly, toothy smile set the ridiculous, misinformed butterflies in her stomach into motion as an image of a

Robert-like face overlaid the familiar, furry one in her mind. "Self-deception is so very easy for the so-inclined," she said, lifting his paw from around her waist by two fingers and letting it drop out of proximity to her. She scooted to the edge of his lap and made to stand.

"Ouch." He gave an exaggerated flinch but made no move to stop her, helping her instead. A church bell chimed a quarter after eleven, and they both stilled. *Spells are midnight things.* Would the castle move without them? Or would whatever building Beast was in move? If the tower moved instead of the castle, Lyndon's approaching help would go to the wrong place.

The church bell continued to peal its tuneful warning. In the silence after it, Beast sniffed. Boots scraped against the stone floor beyond the door—a door with a window in it looking directly toward the wall of empty shackles.

Belinda's heart leapt to her throat as Beast pushed her off him and bounded clumsily to his feet, taking up his old, stretched position in the tangle of shadow and light. She crawled under the light's path to the darkness beside the door. Holding the shackles in his fisted hands, Beast let his head hang down.

A rounded, head-shaped shadow moved over Beast, then retreated. The lock rattled, but the thump of boots against stone retreated. Letting out a great sigh, Beast sank to the floor, his ankles still shackled.

Without thinking about it, Belinda found herself nestled against his side, her shoulder pressed against his, her arms hugging his. "How often do they check on you?" she asked.

"Every half hour or so, I think. I was ... thinking on other things and not paying them much attention."

Hearing the pain in his voice, she squeezed his arm tighter and laid her head on his shoulder.

He pressed his hand over hers and stared at the door, his brows a furry, almond line across his forehead.

"We can't go out that way," she said. "There's a shaft from here up to the old torture chamber at the top of the tower. We can hide there until Lyndon arrives with help, or we can go out the tower window. You can climb the shaft, can't you?"

"Yes ..." The touch of his fingers over hers lightened, and something about his stillness set her at unease. "Belinda," he said slowly. "You know who I am, don't you?"

The cold weight of the golden vase in her satchel pressed against her leg, sending an icy shot to her heart. Belinda stiffened. Sitting up, she pulled her arms from around his.

"I see that you do," he said sadly. Out of the corner of her eye she saw him hesitate, then curve his arm as if to fit it around her. But she was no daughter of a duke.

Belinda scooted forward to his feet and ran her fingers lightly over the plum-sized lock holding his shackles together, ignoring the soft brush of fabric as Beast lowered his arm back to his side. Her heart twisted at his sigh, but one of them at least had to be sensible, and she certainly didn't have time for such sentimental nonsense as wishing she were his equal in rank. She gave the shackles an experimental shove toward his ankles. They barely moved.

Behind, she sensed more than saw Beast examining his hands. "This had better be temporary. By the time my feet shrink enough to get through those shackles, they won't support me."

She pushed up from the floor and brushed rust and dust off her hands. "Which is why we're not using it on them." She stalked around the sizable cell with its several molded straw ticks, bending to peer into corners warded by sticky webs and to peek into nooks and crannies in the walls.

Dust, cobwebs, and the occasional lizard or mouse skeleton

littered the unkempt room. Belinda let out a breath at the sight of such ordinary, possibly useful things, and turned back to Beast. He was staring at her, and though she couldn't tell what he might be thinking, her feminine vanity couldn't help but be pleased.

"You look a bit … bigger than before," Beast said.

So much for vanity.

Self-consciously, Belinda drew her thick cloak closer about her. "Lady Violetta padded my guard uniform to make me look more authentic." She'd neglected to add weapons, to Belinda's chagrin.

"Ah. Clever. I may have to reconsider my opinion of her. She's only *sometimes* lacking in sense." Sitting parallel to the wall, he drew his knees up as much as the chains allowed and rubbed his calf muscles. "By the way, I knew that Lady Violetta recruited you *after* you'd arrived. I was rather angry for a time when I thought she'd sent you. But I'm glad you told me yourself."

"You … you don't blame me for trying?"

"No. You wouldn't be the only one." A rueful smile crept into his voice. "Lyndon never stops. What are you hunting for?"

Belinda squatted in front of a stone block with a chink missing at its base, but that didn't mean the spot was empty. "A key."

"And you think a spider used it to decorate his web?"

"I'm not actually looking for that kind of key. I'm looking for—*aha*—a *skeleton* key." She took out a pinky-sized dropper bottle from a hidden pocket in her satchel and carefully dropped three drops each on her thumb and index finger. She picked up a dusty lizard skeleton of appropriate size, blew it off, and drew it through her moistened fingers. Cupping it into her palm, she hurried back to Beast. She opened her fist before him with a flourish. A short, stout bone-white key lay in her palm. A sparkle lit her eyes as she held it up for Beast's observation.

"You're acquainted with the art of prestidigitation, I see," he said in a voice trying and failing to be unimpressed.

"How can you look at yourself and still be amazed at magic? How could you not expect it?" Laughing as she knelt beside his feet, she slipped the key into the rusty lock at his ankle. The strain on the key as she turned thrummed into her fingers. *Hold up. Just a little more.* The key clicked into place and slid smoothly round. The shackles fell off.

"Just illogical, I suppose." Beast stared at the shackles and then at his ankles, which he rotated and stretched. "You have another one of those for the door?"

She shook her head as the key fell into a pile of tiny, intricate bones in her palm. "It'd take a former prisoner's femur to survive that lock—we're all alone. And it doesn't work on fresh bone," she added with a significant look, as if to forestall any suggestions from Beast.

"Pity. I could've called a guard in. What's your plan then? I hope it involves rescuing Robert as well, for I'm not leaving without him."

"Not yet. We daren't go through the tower—don't try to talk me into it. One sleeping dart and you're out. We go through the shaft, then hide in the chamber or go out the tower window—don't growl at me, unless you want another nice long nap. We'll fetch Robert when help arrives. I know a very respectable, kind-faced matron of the village who would gladly bake sleeping potion–laced snacks for the guards and probably even a cake with an iron file for the bars."

Having wisely ceased growling, Beast *hmm*-ed in appreciation. "How big is this tower window?"

Belinda sketched it out in the air.

"I'll never fit through that, not even with the shrinking

potion." Expectation and curiosity lit his blue eyes as they sought her out again.

Absurd butterflies. "I wouldn't dream of subjecting you once more to the torture of greasy fur." Peering into the inside pocket of her open satchel, she hunted through a stash of bottles and jars, two of which held the voice-activated wardrobe changes. With an exclamation of success, she plucked out a thin, green vial reminiscent of a sapling trapped in glass. "For this, I have a temporary bending potion. For the bars and walls."

His eyes cut from the bottle to the ceiling above, as if it were the window, strayed to Belinda, then down to the glow radiating from the open satchel. Belinda's heart thumped a little harder. *You could fit if you weren't cursed.* "You'll fit. One way or the other."

Beast said nothing.

Belinda replaced the vial and stood, glancing around the coal-black ceiling for the shaft. Lifting the vase above her head, the rose providing an ominous crimson light, she took slow steps around the room. A scrambling noise came from behind her, claws against stone. Her heart ached at the thought of how weakened from the sleeping dart and the torturous stretching of his muscles Beast must be if he were having trouble getting up.

"Sit back down," she ordered. "We aren't going anywhere yet."

"Yet? But—"

"Lady Violetta's order. We have to wait until the shrinking spell wears off your hands. We don't want to fall down the shaft." Like a metronome set at *allegro*, Belinda's heart hammered at the idea even though her head saw its reason. They had to wait, yet they had to be out by midnight. "Something about magic resetting itself, or spells needing time to set, or something." At least that's what she thought Lady

Violetta had murmured. She didn't quite trust the enchantress's cunning look.

A sigh accompanied a thud as Beast settled back onto the floor. She continued her search of the ceiling. On the far side of the lengthy cell, the charcoal stone above her head was replaced by weathered wood and black iron. Standing on tiptoe, she stretched up to push against the trapdoor. Naught but cold air brushed her fingers.

"You might help me open this, though."

"Gladly." Beast pushed himself up, pressing a hand on the wall for support until his legs steadied. He straightened, shook himself like a dog after a swim, then marched over. His claws scratched lightly against the wood as he traced the edges of the square hatch above him before sinking into the wood around the metal bands. He wiggled the hatch up and down. "Will your silence spell extend to this?"

"Yes." If she told it to. She quickly did, grateful for Beast's forethought.

"Good." Stepping away from the hatch, he jerked his chin toward the empty wall by the shackles. "Keep an eye out on the door, will you? I don't want to ram this into your head on accident." Beast flicked his wrists. Curved nails as long as Belinda's hand shot from his fingertips.

When she was safely at his former spot, Beast sank his claws into the wooden hatch and began pulling it slowly down.

"You're not going to just tear it out?"

He snorted as he moved his hands closer to the edges and sank his claws into the wood there. "That would be the beastly thing to do, wouldn't it? Rip out the hatch and go roaring up the shaft." The hatch shifted, but only by a hair. Grimacing as if under a strain, he slowly pulled it downward. "Fortunately, your presence has so far civilized this beast as to make him realize that roaring up would only get him a headache when he crashed into the hatch above." A strip of blackness an inch wide grew above the hatch's far rim. "If I can force this one open, it might trigger the mechanism and open the one above. Then we can go roaring up." Four more inches of darkness appeared.

"What you're saying is that I've made you into a crafty beast?"

Beast laughed, then said softly, "I have a feeling you could make me into more than that." He grunted as the hatch snapped open. Belinda's exclamation of success was cut off by the sound of him slapping his hands together. He squeezed around the open hatch to her. "That would have been so much easier if my hands matched the size of my arms."

"They'll revert soon, I'm sure." They had to.

After a brief check of the door, Beast moved back toward the shackles. He caught Belinda's arm as she went to examine the shaft. "Sit with me. Your hands were affected as well."

Having no reason to object that wouldn't embarrass her, Belinda let him seat her gently beside himself against the wall, the door across. He draped his arm around her shoulders and tucked her against him even as he watched the door.

You know who I am, don't you? The question pinged painfully through Belinda's heart, each echo in a different voice: his mother, his father, Lucrezia, even Robert and Lady Violetta, her own father. Sarcastic, forbidding, shocked.

They sat there quietly, Belinda stiff yet unwilling to move. But the steady rise and fall of Beast's chest finally lulled her out of her stiffness, and she relaxed against him. What were a few stolen minutes of friendship? Everyone was equal in a dungeon.

"I have a limp," Beast said suddenly.

The echoes began again. *Yes, I know. Everyone knows.*

He sighed heavily. "Not as a beast, obviously. Beast is

whole, strong, and heals rapidly. But in my true form, I'm not so fortunate."

"You don't stay a beast to avoid a limp?"

"Beast can get you out of here, but not the limping Prince Rupert," he said with a bitter self-pity Belinda knew better than to answer.

When she didn't respond, he leaned his head back against the wall with another sigh. "For a while, yes. I have an older cousin—I'm sure you've heard of him."

Belinda nodded, her stomach twisting at the image of Robert with a knife in his side.

"Everyone sings his praises. Deservedly so. When I was eight and had been riding a horse a few years, he let me on an unbroken stallion. He thought I was as tough as he had been at that age. He's always had a foolish belief in my abilities. I didn't last three seconds. I was thrown from the horse and suffered a broken leg. It never healed properly, and I developed a limp. I think it put as much of a hitch in my soul as in my step. I worked so hard to overcome my weakness, to be the best at whatever I was assigned—archery, hand-to-hand combat, swordplay, politics and economics. But Robert always beat me, as did many others. I grew stronger for the beatings and the challenge, but they weren't easy to take.

"When I was twenty-one, my father, Robert, I, and many of the nobles went on a hunting trip in one of the more remote areas of the kingdom. We were ambushed. I took an arrow to the shoulder trying to protect my father. Robert took an arrow as well, but he also knocked my father off his horse into the shelter of a small hollow. Father was unharmed, Robert was well in two days, and I ..." He paused, then took a deep breath. "I was confined to bed for a month. My injury became infected, and my arm, like my leg, lost some of its strength. But even before that, after I took the arrow for my father, as I lay in the dirt and leaves, bleeding and in agony,

Father was yelling at me for endangering myself—the heir who should be protected.

"He was concerned for me," Beast hastily continued at Belinda's indignant gasp. "He doesn't handle fear for his loved ones well." He smiled wanly. "I don't take concern well. Or failure."

Impressions of Beast, like strokes in a painting, came together in Belinda's mind. The enchantress's description of him as an indolent, self-absorbed Beast. Beast's own claims to laziness and frivolity but sneaking of kingdom-business books when he thought she wasn't watching, his care for his servants and her. The two letters, the better discarded. "You gave up, didn't you, for a time?"

"Yes." He said it with a blandness that suggested his mind had gone back to the moment when caring had ceased and neither pain nor purpose mattered. It held a gray sound Belinda understood far too well. She tugged his slightly small hand into her lap, and he shook himself.

"Yes," he repeated, shame in his tone. "I saw the strain being king put on my father, the burdens he bore. I saw the people's love of my cousin, so strong and whole and confident. I saw myself, bedridden again, never good enough—so I thought: what good was I if not first and best in everything? —destined to a life of responsibility and hardship I wasn't fit for. So I gave up. Books were my comfort when I was ill, when I was sore and struggling to walk after a day's training, so I clung to them. I became an indolent prince who lived for nothing but books and tea cakes and quiet firesides. That I was good at being. Father would certainly get fed up sooner or later and name Robert his heir. We could each be what we were good at."

"It's your kingdom," she said quietly, "whether you limp or not, it's yours. You don't get to choose your calling."

"Robert would be a good king."

Belinda poked Beast in the side. "You know your father arranged the curse to snap you out of your melancholy, right? You'd be a good king too. The kingdom's always thought so."

Beast rubbed his side with a mock glare at her. "I figured out about the curse soon enough, about the same time I realized Father would never give the kingdom to Robert. He'd give it to Robert's sister's toddler rather than Robert just to spite my plans. Even if he did, Robert would reject it to spite me as well."

"Good for them."

"Traitor."

Belinda shrugged and snuggled back against him. She fancied a fond smile twitched his lips before he continued, his arm hugging her to his side again. "It was also about that time I realized I could be of use as Beast."

Her own smile flattened out. "The mirror."

"For a time, I can do more for my kingdom as a beast than a prince."

For a time ...

Her hopeful question vanished as he suddenly released her. "Speaking of Beast, we should hurry. My hands just started itching. I'm hoping that's a good sign."

Belinda hoped so too, for her own sake as well.

Holding up one hand, Beast traced his palm and wrist and on down his forearm, as if feeling their size, then nodded as if pleased. He stood and offered her his hand. She reached for it, but he suddenly drew it back. He locked gazes with her, and something about his earnest stare made her heart ache.

Please don't ask me.

Please do.

"I said all that, Belinda," he said, his eyes intent on hers, "to say this: I can't give up the curse yet—not even for you. Especially not for you. I need it to get us out. Even then, I'm not through with it yet. The kingdom needs it."

Yet.

For you.

For a moment all Belinda saw was blue, and it was beautiful. Then a gray haze dulled the blue of promise and of hope of a love returned into the royal blue of blood too far above her own. Such hopes were too good for her. She knew better than to dream of wonderful things for herself.

Beast held out his hand to her, and she hesitated.

"Belinda ...?"

The chime proclaiming the quarter hour vibrated through the tower stones ... once ... twice ... three times.

Belinda bounded up, clasped Beast's hand, and dragged him toward the shaft, its open hatch blocking nearly half of the room's width.

Catching her urgency without the need for words, Beast let her tow him until scooting around her in front of the hatch. He knelt, his back to her. "May I offer you the breadth of my back, my lady?"

Halting in pulling a rope from her satchel, Belinda looked askance at him, then up the seemingly sheer tunnel, and let her shoulders fall in defeat of pride. "Riding piggyback is so indecorous," she grumbled as she replaced the rope. She clasped her arms around Beast's neck. "I am not five years old, you know."

Beast shifted her arms away from his throat and rose slowly. "Indecorous depends on your culture. And I've never known you to let that stop you before."

"I thought a gentleman always agreed with a lady."

He stepped back, then leapt onto the wall, catching its stone with his claws, and began climbing up the tunnel with the ease of a spider. "I'm a beast."

Feeling her heart was out of its proper position, Belinda swallowed hard to push it back to its home before managing a reply. "I thought there was something different about you beyond the extra hair."

Beast chuckled.

Stone ruffled her cloak, and Belinda flattened against Beast. She sensed more than saw his careful searching of the rock above for handholds in the pitch black. For a moment, she thought she heard a commotion below, but it was probably only the echo of Beast's claws on the stone.

"Do Beasts not see in the dark?"

"Not in this grade of darkness. Hold on."

She stifled a gasp as he swung back, twisting until his free arm reached her satchel. He pushed the flap back. A crimson glow dulled the darkness.

"There." He swung back around, grasping the wall with both hands before reaching for a higher hold.

Belinda let out a breath, but it didn't grant the relief she anticipated. She didn't like to admit it, but she wasn't terribly fond of heights. Not terribly afraid, but not terribly fond.

"What are you hoping to find using the mirror?" she asked as a distraction.

"I'm not quite sure. The man who tried to shoot my father was killed before he could tell who hired him. A bottle of poison was found in his pocket, but we didn't think it'd been used on the arrows, since Robert and I lived. At some point, though, it dawned on me that the arrow meant for my father *had* been poisoned, but with a potion of some kind. I'd always thought there was something odd about my illness after taking the arrow. It wasn't entirely a festering wound.

"With my servants' help, I used the mirror to hunt for and watch every known enemy of my father, every maker of poisons and any enchanter or enchantress with a checkered past, determined to find who tried to poison my father and prevent any more attempts. We've actually managed to stop a number of attempted poisonings and deal with the guilty, but we found nothing concerning my father."

"But when I looked at the mirror—"

"It showed the Duke of Marblue. After much research and with Lyndon's help, I discovered what the poison was: a suggestion potion. Some have to be mixed with blood to work, hence the arrow. Whoever it was tied to—the one who could make the suggestion—must not have reached me to enact it. Before the attack, Father had been after me to marry, and Lucrezia had been rather hinting I should marry her, as we'd grown up together. I told her no in no uncertain terms," he added quickly, and Belinda wasn't sure whether to be pleased or distressed that he wanted her to know that. "If my father thought he was seriously injured, he'd insist on my marrying immediately."

"And if the duke visited him, he would suggest Lucrezia as the bride."

"Exactly."

"But I'd always heard the Duke of Marblue was a very loyal man. I can't imagine him endangering your father."

"Marblue would give his right arm for the kingdom while strangling it with his left. He's a harsh ruler to his own people, but a good adviser in some areas, and loyal, as you say. But from listening in on his conversations, he apparently believes he's destined to have a king as a grandson. It was prophesied by a fairy at Lucrezia's birth or something like that. Being very loyal as you say, he's determined his grandson will be king of New Beaumont."

Unconsciously, Belinda tightened her hold possessively around Beast, then blushed and loosened it when Beast responded, "Don't worry. *She* will never be queen of New Beaumont."

That *she* set off a host of different reactions, so it was not soon enough, to Belinda's mind, that they reached the rough wood of the top hatch. Beast hauled them out onto the solid stone floor. Dust flew up in greeting, or in a warning to stay away. They were back in the chamber she'd stopped at on her way to Beast. Window, stairs under the man-sized cage, broken instruments of torture. It wasn't an inviting room.

Belinda rolled off Beast's back and pushed to her feet, her stomach not giving up its twists despite the solidness of rock under her feet.

"I'll find the chains that close the trapdoors," Beast said as he rose. "Maybe they'll assume a good fairy spirited me away if they see no obvious exit. You get the bending potion for the window ready."

Belinda pulled a rope with a three-pronged claw on one end from her satchel and eyed the window high above even the cage's stairs. She jogged up the stairs until she was opposite the window. A fall of twenty feet or so loomed between the window and the chamber floor, a short distance compared to what lay between the window and the street. Her stomach cinched. She was *not* afraid of heights. Others might be, but not Belinda Lambton.

Swinging the grappling hook back and forth, testing its weight, she judged the distance to the window, then let the rope fly. Metal clanged against metal as the hook caught the window bars. She made her way gingerly back down the stairs and stood under the window, rope in sweaty hand. Her muscles felt like putty on fire just looking up to the window. Life at a castle was very bad for the muscles required for daring rescues.

She jumped at the deep, rumbly voice beside her. "May I take part in this rescue?" Beast snagged the rope from her grasp.

"You have already," she rasped between unusually noticeable heartbeats. "You're the cause of it."

"All the more reason for you to hand over the potion."

She was only too glad to do so, and to watch, by moonlight and rose glow, as Beast climbed agilely up the wall to the window. In that moment, she could understand him keeping his curse.

Crouching at the window ledge, he used his handkerchief to smear the bending potion over the bars and walls. "I smell Marigold down there, and Stargazer."

"Naturally." Not for the first time, Belinda felt the pockets of her guard's uniform. No timepiece. How long did they have? "You didn't think I planned to fly back to the castle, did you?"

"It wouldn't be surpr—" He stilled, then sniffed the air again.

The chime of midnight vibrated through the tower stones into her heart. *Remember, Belinda, spells are midnight things.* What did that mean for a curse? For the potions she'd used?

Boots scraped against the stone floor beyond the chamber door.

Belinda's heart leapt to her throat as Beast pushed off from the window, using the rope to swing onto the stairs. He bounded down them, almost flying down to her. He bent in front of her, and she climbed onto his back. With one step back, he leapt onto the wall and began to climb.

Belinda held tight, heart hammering, and blinked as her vision blurred.

The door crashed open against the wall. Torchlight assaulted the chamber's darkness. She prayed that, for once, darkness would advance rather than light. *Don't look up.*

"Belinda." Beast's voice was grave, hesitant, yet seemed strangely far away. She concentrated on steadying her breathing, unwilling to let fear steal her senses. "Is your silence spell still working?"

Focusing on her ears, she felt again a slight tingle there. "Yes."

"Good. I—Belinda, it's a new day now. ... I'm sure you know that means I must ask you something."

Her heart stuttered. "Yes, Beast."

"I want you to ... not answer—not yet."

A village girl can never answer. Not truly answer.

"And I don't mean refuse through silence. You will answer, won't you, when I ask you to?"

Belinda nodded against his back.

"Belinda Lambton, will you marry me?"

Belinda buried her face against his back and said nothing. Rather, she listened to the shouts below, to the clamor of men and the commands of a woman as they neared.

"See how the shadows change!"

"Up there!"

Beast stopped climbing. She opened her eyes to meet the window's moonlit gaze.

"Can you reach the rope?" Beast clutched the stones framing the window, the rock gently bending under his weight.

Shaking her head to clear her vision, she cautiously reached out with one hand. As her fist secured the rope, she slipped off Beast, caught herself on the rope, and planted her feet against the wall. She, the rope, and the wall all dipped. Beast held his arm protectively beneath her. Biting her lip, she focused on her grip on the rope. She hadn't really considered that angle of the bending potion. When the potion-lathered wall came to rest on an unbending portion, she planted her feet against the wall, and Beast shifted back to the window.

Crouching on its frame, he pulled on the rusted iron bars, bending them like licorice until they touched the stone walls, which gave way to let them bend even more.

"This is the part," he said, his tone half jesting and half

tense, "where you're supposed to clasp your hands over your heart and bat your eyelashes and exclaim how strong I am."

At least that's what she thought he said. It was difficult to hear anything over the pounding of her heart and the wind howling outside the window. And she was so tired.

Beast stuck his head out the window, his shoulders filling the opening. "It's too far. The rope will never reach." The words carried back in on the frigid breeze, one that made her vision blur again, though cold air usually woke her.

"Beast! Come down!" Lucrezia didn't need to yell. The command was clear even to Belinda's tired mind. "My guards are already surrounding the tower. You can't escape."

"Climb out after me and be quick. You'll have to hold on to me," Beast hissed. "We'll go over the rooftops." He squirmed between the bars and disappeared.

Belinda tried to follow. One sluggish hand moved over the other, once, twice. She shook her head as she grabbed the stone ledge framing the window. Why was she so tired? She had to follow Beast out.

Out.

One sharp message shot through the fog in her mind as her vision blurred. Beast was going out to the village in the early morning. Spells were midnight things. The curse thought it was Beast's daily jaunt.

It thought it was time for her to dream.

An image of Beast back in the tower, kneeling for Belinda to climb onto his back blurred the starry, rooftop-silhouetted sky beyond the window.

"Bea—!" Belinda went limp.

CHAPTER 17

"**B**east!" *Belinda's dream self finished the cry.*

But the Beast she saw wouldn't understand. He thought Belinda safe on his back as he climbed up the wall, the window in view. Blasted time delay! Would she be late for her own death?

"I want you to ... not answer—not yet," Beast told her.

Could she answer him at all now? Lyndon said she talked in her dream-filled sleep, but when? In her time or the dream's delayed time?

As Beast squeezed through the window, Belinda's dream self caught the light of torches crossing the room. Lucrezia and seven guards, one with an elegant air about his unusually tall and lithe form, ran for the window. They reached the wall under it as a scream assaulted the air.

She watched in horror as her sleeping form plummeted toward guards with raised swords, all quickly backing away to uncover solid stone.

Lucrezia stood watching, as frozen as Belinda, one hand covering her mouth, the other clutching her stomach. For one brief moment, Belinda thought that maybe, just maybe, the duke's daughter had some unselfish instincts.

Beast shot back through the window, his paws touching the wall once, using it as a spring board to dive for her. He caught her cloak and yanked her to him. He pushed off the wall again, twisting his body under hers as they fell. He smashed into an old table beyond the soldiers. It collapsed under him, and he lost his grip on her. She rolled away to the trapdoor. Her feet lay on the stone floor, but the rest of her sprawled across groaning wood.

Six guards, swords drawn, surrounded Beast as he struggled to his knees, swaying as if dazed. The tallest guard bowed slightly to Lucrezia, his gaze seeming to bore into hers. He gestured to Beast. "Your prisoner, my lady."

A shiver passed over Lucrezia, and she pressed her hand over a locket. Her stance changed, as if that shiver were a transformation from a caring woman into the Lucrezia Belinda knew.

Lucrezia brushed past the soldier. "I told you I'd be back in the morning, Beast. How rude of you not to wait for me." She smiled her saccharine smile at Beast, but her elegant gown whisked over dusty stone toward Belinda. She stopped several feet back, a look of horror on her face as she reached out a hand toward Belinda, but she quickly drew back, her posture stiffening. The regal guard sauntered past her and toed Belinda in the shoulder. The trapdoor dipped under the pressure. With a look at him, Lucrezia spun away and strolled, her pace one of contained speed, to the guards surrounding the still-dazed Beast. She lifted her chin. "And to try running away with that."

Belinda wondered if it were possible to haunt in her dream form. It would almost make dying separate from her body worth it. Almost.

Wake up, Belinda! Wake up!

But she couldn't so much as make her sleeping self blink.

Beast's swaying stilled, his head swiveling toward Lucrezia's voice, then away. His gaze snapped to Belinda, and he bolted to his feet. The burly guards shoved him down. He slipped on splinters of the busted table and crashed to the floor again.

"For pity's sake, Lucrezia, help her!" Beast yelled. "Get her away from there!" Six blades pressed into his filthy velvet suit as he tried to *stand. "Please, Lucrezia." Hands raised, he slowly pushed himself up. "What's happened to you?"*

Lucrezia paled, and she tugged on the locket hanging about her neck. "Beast, I—"

Cocking his head to study Belinda, the guard toed her again. "She's tied to your curse, isn't she? Like my lady."

Beast's shocked look at the insolent guard ended in a narrow-eyed glare. "Not by my choice." He focused on Lucrezia again. "Get her away from there, please, Lucrezia. Tell your men to leave her alone."

Lucrezia smiled, her lips faltering once before sticking to their place. Had the twisted woman any natural, genuine smiles left in her? "No."

"She's more useful as she is." The tall guard rattled the trapdoor with his polished black boot, a placid smile stretching his thin lips as he raised an eyebrow in challenge to Beast.

With a growl, Beast lunged at the gap between his guards, but six swords refused him passage. One guard kicked him in the knees, throwing him off balance as he tried to steady himself on the table debris.

"You can't help her if you're impaled, Beast dear." Lucrezia gave him a cunning look. "Strategically impaled so you'll be recovered by our wedding."

Beast stilled.

"Oh yes. I know all about your curse," Lucrezia said, an edge of acerbity in her voice. "All about its healing properties, its rules and its quirks, its rose and its end. How no other spell can touch you. I read the spell's entire entry, which is probably more than you or that imbecile Lady Violetta can say."

Beast's gaze shot down to his left hand, then to the rose in Belinda's open satchel. A spark of hope flickered across his face. He lowered his hands. "You can't force me to propose, Lucrezia. Not anymore."

Her smile faltered, confusion tugging at it. She looked to that elegant guard, walking so calmly and stately around the chamber, trying the different chains, watching the trapdoor as he did. "You must," she said. "It's part of the curse."

Beast shook his head.

"But the rose's petals will drop if you disobey it." Her eyes caught on the red glow leaking from the leather satchel to give Belinda an eerie halo.

"Curses have rules—and a sense of honor." Beast lifted his left hand. A flash of red and green and gold twined about his ring finger, flaring once before settling into his fur to rest against his skin. A similar band encircled Belinda's finger. "I asked Belinda to marry me, because I had to"—he looked past Lucrezia to Belinda lying still on the wood and smiled that hideous, beautiful smile of his—"because I wanted to."

Crossing her arms, Lucrezia stepped between them, blocking Beast's view.

His glare at her softened into an expression almost pitying. "I meant the question, Lucrezia. I asked, but she hasn't answered yet. I can't ask you or anyone else until she does. She won't wake until I've returned to the castle. You've no reason to keep us. After she answers, just as now, you've no hope of me proposing to you, or anyone else, ever again. She will say yes."

He looked at Belinda, his mouth forming silent words. Her ears tingled, and Beast's mouth began to move again with sound. She heard him, but she didn't. He'd called for her silencing spell. "I know she will," he said to her alone. "No foolish, pride-based definition of what a suitable match is will stop her. She's too wise and too brave for that." He took a step toward her. "Please, Belinda. Say yes. I love you."

The guards tightened their circle around him, watching him warily.

"Leave now," he said aloud to them all. "If Robert heals with no ill effects, I won't even seek justice against you and your father. If you leave us now."

The guards twitched their blades at him, giving one another looks of wariness, and possibly self-protecting murder.

Lucrezia opened her mouth, shut it, and clutched at her locket again. "Father had nothing to do with this," she spat. "You wouldn't cooperate, so I did what was necessary. It was prophesied I'd bear a king, so both you and the curse can forget about your village twit—and your stupid honor. I had to!" Her color rising, she yanked at the locket's chain so hard Belinda was sure it'd snap, but it didn't. She threw her hand away from it in a manner fit for a tantrum, her glare momentarily searing into the placid face of the wandering guard. He patted his pocket, then reached to test another rusted chain. She spun back around to a bewildered Beast.

"I'm not the only prince in the world," Beast said.

"You're the prince of New Beaumont. Why would I want to be queen of anywhere else? This is my home and my people. My fate. To defy fate would be to destroy the kingdom! Do you want that?" She flicked her gaze toward Belinda and the guard. She stepped closer, her voice lowering. "If you care, you'll cease this foolishness and ask me." Her eyes went deadly serious. "Quickly, Rupert."

Beast's jaw went slack as he looked between her and the unearthly, elegant guard. "What have you done, Lucrezia?"

"There's no rush, my lady." The guard wrapped long, thin fingers around a chain stretching up to a mechanism set into the wall. He tugged the chain and released it. Belinda's sleeping form bounced as the trapdoor dipped and snapped shut again. He smiled. "We've plenty of time."

Beast went down in a tangle of guards before Belinda's dream self even saw him move. "Wake up, Belinda! Wake up!" His shout went silent to all but her as he fought the guards.

Lucrezia stared about her as if the world had gone mad. She backed away as Beast launched one guard, his sword bloody, from the circle. A matching line of red ran down Beast's side. She stared at it. "Please, Rupert! Say you'll marry me and relinquish the curse. For the kingdom, if not for me—we were always friends." She yanked again at the golden chain about her neck. "I was raised to be queen," she cried, her voice growing hysterical. "Our fathers expect us to marry.

We have to! Please ask and no one will be hurt. Everyone—even Robert—will be well."

From the tangle of guards, Beast cried, *"Wake up, Belinda! Answer me now! You promised to answer!"*

"Oh, but you can't rely on that," said the tall guard with a sinister smoothness to his voice. *"Can you, my lady?"* He grasped the chain with both hands and jerked it as dream Belinda cried out her answer, all her heart in it.

But the Belinda Beast saw was silent.

He burst through the wall of guards and sprinted for her. *"Wake up, Belinda! Answer! Will you marry me—Prince Rupert of New Beaumont? I take back my crown!"*

The trapdoor slammed into the tunnel wall. Without its support, Belinda crumpled and fell into the shaft.

"I relinquish my curse! Say yes, Belinda, and wake!" Beast dove for the tunnel.

Dream Belinda stilled, then screamed as the pull of gravity yanked her down and air rushed through her hair. Her vision split and sped. Half as if from her sleeping self and half from her dream self, each set of images moving too quickly for life: Beast dove. The tall guard snapped his fingers. Beast collapsed with a roar of pain and disappeared in a burst of violet. It exploded through the room, flattening the soldiers and Lucrezia, slamming the tall guard against the wall.

Belinda's sleeping self caught in the air and hung in the shaft in a blaze of crimson and gold that rose to burst into the chamber and overtake it. A blossoming vine of red and green and gold sealed itself about her finger. Her satchel rose into the air, pulling her along. Violet light broke all around her as tunnel gave way to chamber. The rose and vase floated from her satchel toward the blaze surrounding Prince Rupert.

One crimson petal after another slipped from the rose to shift to fur and vanish into the stone. As the last petal fell, the rose disap-

peared, and the rainbow-play of light around Prince Rupert vanished.

Time began to slow from its frenzied pace. Belinda crashed to the stone a few feet from the trapdoor. This time she felt the pain and heard her own gasp as she hit.

CHAPTER 18

Belinda's vision merged. A stone ceiling high above, men moving all around. Sounds of chaos. Guards yelled as they pushed up from the floor. The chamber door crashed open once again. Robert staggered in, sword in hand and waist wrapped in a bloodied bandage. Winthrop and Lettie—wide-eyed and clutching a slipping and sliding two-layered chocolate cake to her chest like a lifeline to her former life—pushed in after him. A dozen villagers armed with non-standard weapons followed. They scattered as more guards in the Duke of Marblue's uniform swarmed in.

Pushing up to her elbows, her arms trembling, Belinda looked around for Beast—Rupert. Between the dashing feet of guards and villagers, she saw him, lying on the floor, unmoving, looking oddly small despite his height and muscular build. Beast's clothes swallowed him like a father's coat did a child. "Prince Rupert!" *It's your turn to wake up, Beast!*

"Kill the prince or he'll hang you all," the tall guard shouted, a strange authority to his voice. "And catch the duke's daughter before they do!"

Guards and villagers alike paused to stare at him.

"Don't listen to him! You've lost!" Belinda yelled, trying and failing to get her feet to work. She got her knees underneath her, then one foot, then she crashed back to the floor, letting out a scream of pain and frustration. As if a switch had been flipped with that shriek, everyone surged into motion again.

Lucrezia snatched up a dropped sword as two guards lunged for her. Several men sprang toward Rupert, including Robert, his movements slow and puppet-like, as if every muscle were straining. He was still greenish and deathly pale.

"Robert, no!" Belinda screamed.

He staggered to the side as he hunched his shoulder to his ear. "Rupert! Get up, you bloody idiot! Kick me! Do something!" he bellowed as his sword jerked up as if of its own accord. "Lucrezia! Belinda! Help us!"

Getting both feet underneath her, Belinda attempted to spring up and found herself aided by two guards as they grabbed her arms. "Rupert, move!" she cried.

The prince moaned and rolled to his side. Robert's sword waved in a crazed fashion, then swung. "Move!" he bellowed again as his sword sliced down.

A meaty fist grabbed Robert's collar and hurled him to the floor. Robert's sword clattered to the stone. Gaspard's uncle, who was closer to fitting Beast's clothes than any there, seized Robert by the jacket and ploughed a way through the melee, dragging the unconscious Robert with him.

Belinda silently blessed the man as she kicked the guards holding her. Ignoring the assault as pathetic, they lifted her by the arms and forced her toward the unearthly guard.

"Belinda! We're coming!" Winthrop, his goal of getting Lettie through the crowd to a safe corner of the room not going so well, swiveled around toward Belinda, and nearly ran into a guard sparring with a villager. He kicked the guard in the back of the knee and swiftly spun Lettie, cake and all, in one direction as she tried to dart in another. "Just a moment!" he yelled. Lettie yelped as they ducked a swinging sword and dodged the long handle of a pitchfork. Winthrop pulled Gaspard's pistol from his belt and used his long arm to rap the butt over a guard's head, momentarily clearing a path.

"Put me down!" Belinda growled, kicking her feet, but only managing to get them more and more tangled in her cloak. "I call forth Costume Number Two!" she yelled. *Please, let it come with weapons and no cloak.*

A poof of vibrant colors, mostly shades of violet with silver sparkles, surrounded her. An airy chill swept over her skin, and she suddenly understood the necessity of the bright, concealing flashes of light during transformations. *Please, let this one have weapons.* The light vanished with a thunderclap and sparkle.

Belinda reached for her side and touched only gauzy fabric. She choked as she held out her bare arms above the carriage-wide, violet gown now billowing out around her.

Of all the ridiculous—

She could complain later. Where were her guards?

The two men lay sprawled on the floor just beyond the gauzy violet fabric like felled bowling pins.

Had her dress ...?

They stared at her, wide-eyed, not attempting to get up. Too shocked. She could understand that.

She yanked up fistfuls of skirt and darted between them. And tripped on fine fabric.

But her voluminous skirt did stop her from hitting the stone.

Her skirt and two guards.

"Are you all right, my lady?" they asked as they righted her. Their tone was concerned, their eyes approving ... and seeking approval.

I wouldn't be fit to marry him.

You would if you were wearing one of my dresses.

Do they enchant people to approve of you?

Belinda grinned a wicked grin, then hid it behind one of her sweetest, coupling it with a doe-eyed look as she gently broke from their hold. "Oh, thank you, gentlemen. I don't know what I would have done without you. I'm trying to get over there." She raised an elegantly jeweled hand to Rupert. "To him. Would you be so kind as to help me?"

"Of course, my lady!"

"Anything for you!"

Belinda sent another wicked grin to Winthrop and Lettie as they stared at her, an unconscious guard at their feet. She nodded toward the corner of the room, reverently grabbed fistfuls of her dress, and marched after her two admirers, calling out encouragements to them and warnings to the villagers as the soldiers deftly cleared a way to Rupert.

He was still struggling to rise, hampered by Beast's clothes and his need to throw bits of broken table at a steady stream of assailants.

Belinda had a sudden inkling of what Costume Number Three was. "I call forth Costume Number Three," she said quietly, hoping her satchel, now a jeweled bracelet, still held its potions.

Rupert yelped as he was swallowed by a blue thunder-cloud. He reappeared after a blinding flash and a clap of thunder. Belinda's heart did a little flip-flop. *Her Rupert.* She'd agreed, and she wouldn't take it back. He was her prince. And he was beautiful in all ways.

His elegant blue jacket and crisp trousers that fit snugly over an athletic frame certainly didn't hurt that impression any. He looked every bit a handsome prince, and a prince to be reckoned with. *He* had a sword at his side.

Springing to his feet and taking a half-second to steady himself from his limp, he searched the room until his eyes found hers. He looked his thanks and something warmer, then leapt back as a guard swung at him.

His hand fell automatically to his side. His fingers closed around the sword hilt and deftly drew the sword from the heavily decorated scabbard. Out came a long, gleaming, intricately carved showpiece topped with a jeweled hilt. "A *ceremonial* sword?" he bellowed as the jewels caught the light and sparkled. Gritting his teeth, he lunged forward with it anyway. His blade diverted from a chest-ward thrust to a very firm tap on the opposing guard's shoulder. This was swiftly followed with another tap of equal violence on the man's other shoulder and was accompanied by a bewildered look from both Rupert and the guard. Whether by gravity or magic, the man fell to his knees, his sword landing at Rupert's feet as if set there in offering.

Belinda groaned. Seriously? The enchantress was worried about blood spoiling the clothes she'd made?

"What's that, my lady?" her escorts asked, worriedly.

"Nothing! You're doing splendidly!" She picked up her pace, encouraging her guards to do likewise.

Rupert's mouth opened, then closed. "A ceremonial sword ..." he stammered, then rapped the kneeling man over the head with the sword hilt and spun away to knight someone else.

Her guards engaged a couple of soldiers coming in behind Rupert.

Across the room, the tall man yelled, frustration evident despite the commanding smoothness of his voice, "I said to kill him! Stupid mortals. I'll do it myself then!"

"Prince Dokar! Don't! Please!" Lucrezia screamed. She stood over Robert, holding a sword out awkwardly toward an approaching guard. He knocked the sword away and grabbed her wrist.

A chill swept through Belinda. Prince Dokar—the

unearthly guard was the Unseelie Prince, the fairy who delighted in all things malicious—he was the one who'd been aiding Lucrezia? *Almighty, help us.*

Striding through the rapidly parting crowd, Prince Dokar flicked one hand to the side and snapped the fingers of his other. Belinda flew back, away from her guards. They, shaking their heads as if waking, disengaged from the fight. Her dress had lost its vibrancy. Rupert's sword clattered to the ground and turned to ash.

"Lady Violetta!" Belinda cried. "Help! Lady Violetta!"

Ten feet away, Prince Dokar threw back his arm, then drew it forward, a sword, its blade gleaming ebony and etched in runes of bloodred, in his hand.

There was a cry and a commotion beside him as soldiers and villagers scattered, thrusting one another out of the way. Shoved by a guard, Lettie stumbled out from the crowd, Winthrop desperately reaching for her. She staggered into Prince Dokar. With a shriek, she smashed the cake into his face. He screamed as if in pain and vanished in a cloud of thick black. Cake, platter, and a chocolate-covered rod crashed to the floor where he'd been.

As if an order of silence had been given, everyone stilled and stared as Winthrop broke through the crowd. "It's over," he shouted as he drew a trembling Lettie to his chest. "Throw down your weapons."

"They'll hang us all if they take us," a guard shouted. "Get what prisoners you can!"

And the chaos began again.

Belinda, unable to get traction against her layers of petticoats, struggled, helpless, as a guard grabbed her round the waist. Still on his feet, Rupert leapt back over a fallen guard to avoid a blow, landed badly on his weak leg, and fell, two guards now bearing down on him.

"Stop in the king's name!"

CHAPTER 19

"I'm sorry we took so long, my dear."

Lady Violetta, in a gown matching Belinda's, only wider, stood like a violet star in the center of the room. King Patrick, Queen Marianne, Lyndon, and a dozen soldiers grouped around her like obedient planets.

Everyone, villagers included, dropped their weapons. Belinda's guard dropped her.

She landed with a squeal on the stone, but then Rupert was there, lifting her gently up and hugging her to him. She wrapped her arms about him in a fierce hug before pulling away enough to take in the newly arrived.

"I thought you couldn't transport a group of armed men," she said, finding it difficult to sound cross when she was so happy.

Lady Violetta lifted a shoulder in an elegant shrug. "Well," she said, the corner of her mouth curving in a sly smile as she gestured toward her companions, who looked fit for a coronation or wedding. "There's nothing in the rules about not transporting for a ceremony. And as to a group, now that the curse is lifted, I feel years younger." She regarded Belinda a moment, her expression pleased. "You look stunning, dear."

Belinda smiled. "I must remember to thank my seamstress."

Stepping from the circle, King Patrick raised his sword to the nearest of the Duke of Marblue's guards, resting it just beneath the man's chin. He glanced at Rupert. "What now, son?"

Rupert stood a little straighter. "Sir William," he addressed a man with a black physician's bag, "tend Robert and the other wounded. The rest of you, take all those bearing the Duke of Marblue's colors prisoner. The villagers are our friends." He smiled down at Belinda before turning back to his parents. "Father, Mother, come meet your future daughter-in-law."

"What of Lady Lucrezia?" Lyndon asked.

Lucrezia knelt on the floor beside Robert, an empty vial in her lap, her arms wrapped around herself. She looked up at Rupert, her face so stricken Belinda couldn't help pitying her. "He said he'd heal him. Prince Dokar promised no one would get hurt. It was just for show." She rocked forward, stifling a sob. "But you wouldn't cooperate, Rupert. You wouldn't marry me. It was promised. I had to do something." Sniffling, she pushed herself up and faced the king, her hands out in a pleading gesture. "My father didn't know. Prince Dokar and I planned this. Please, don't blame my father. Prince Dokar promised no one would get hurt." With another sob, she fled the room, yanking at the locket whose chain refused to break.

The king's guards looked to him, and after a glance at Rupert, he shook his head.

As the king and queen neared Belinda and Rupert, Lettie, not daring to approach the prince, was busy trying to catch Belinda's eye. She mouthed at her, "Why didn't you tell me your escort was the prince!" She widened her eyes dramatically and grinned at her.

From beside the king, Lyndon winked at Rupert, then nodded toward Belinda.

Rupert caught that wink and wrapped his arms back around Belinda's waist, tugging her to him. "There was something you said earlier," he whispered softly, his mouth by her ear, "that I'd very much like to hear again."

"About what?" Belinda said, finding it very hard to breathe, much less think clearly, with Rupert so close and so very, wonderfully human.

His mouth curved up as he lifted her left hand and kissed her ring finger, where a hint of the red, green, and gold vines still lingered. "I think you know."

Oh.

He tilted her chin up toward him, and Belinda felt the full force of those blue eyes of his, eyes that told her exactly the same thing she wanted to tell him but couldn't say so eloquently. But she had to try. She'd promised to answer—and she'd answer every day for the rest of their lives.

"I—I said yes, that I love yo—"

Apparently getting the gist of her reply, Rupert interrupted her with a kiss.

Though time for Belinda seemed to still in that perfect moment, the rest of the world spun around them, its chaos subsiding, its voices slowly coming back into focus.

"Prince Dokar was here?" Lady Violetta exclaimed, alarmed, as she searched the room. "Where did he go?"

"Vanished. In a powdery poof like that of a kicked mushroom." Winthrop half sat, half collapsed onto the floor and buried his face in his hands. "My wife, my foolishly brave, wonderful wife threw an iron file into the face of Prince Dokar—storybook villain in the flesh. An immortal fairy prince."

Lettie paled and sat down heavily beside him, telltale icing on her dress.

The king and queen, who'd stopped to listen to Winthrop, turned to Lady Violetta. "What can be done to protect them?" the queen asked.

Lady Violetta's mouth opened and closed soundlessly before she shrugged. It wasn't a gesture of elegant indifference this time. "Always carry iron with you? Hope he didn't catch your name or get ahold of anything of yours?" She turned to Belinda. "Belinda dear, what do you think?"

But Belinda wasn't paying attention. Rupert was kissing her. Again.

Crossing her arms, Lady Violetta nodded curtly at Lyndon, who was trying to cover a grin. "Well, let no one say *I* can't bring about a happily-ever-after."

⚜

I HAD a wish to grant by midnight. My own wish to amuse myself. I am a true fairy godfather—I search the mortal lands for one to be my servant, to amuse me with plots for unsettling kit and kin and kingdom. My lady promised fair for a time, and when I say my *lady, I mean it, for that's what she is. Mine. Desperation and fear and ambition, they've gained me much over the millennia. From this woman they brought me a lock of hair in a bargain she didn't understand. She belongs to me now. Everything of hers belongs to me. Her fate. Her control of the young lord. The king she'll one day marry. I didn't lose.*

There are other midnights. Other wishes to grant.

—PRINCE DOKAR, *of the Unseelie Faerie*

A CURSE KEEPER, CURSE BREAKER Fairytale

Robert, Duke of Pondleigh, already has one curse, so what's another one? Or two? If only these things involved fighting monsters—or even being turned into one—he'd be fine. But attempting to force him into marrying the woman who nearly killed him by cursing him to either gain a lady's kiss each day or become a frog, simply isn't gentlemanly. The fact the princess he's been in love with for years won't even answer his letters, much less see him, doesn't help his chances of freedom.

Princess Snow has excellent reasons for going into hiding at the Cottage for Retired Enchanters deep in the New Grimmland forests, reasons like a terrible secret and an overprotective stepmother. When Robert, the duke she thought had forgotten her, shows up as a frog, he seems to think she's his curse breaker, but Snow knows better: her kisses are poison.

With wit and clean romance, Cursed for Keeps is a mashup retelling of "The Frog Prince" and "Snow White and the Seven Dwarfs."

It releases mid-2021.

The Mouse King Has Taken One Crown too Many

Janawyn Stahl is convinced there's a connection between her godfather's suspiciously talkative automaton named Theo and his lost nephew, but can she protect Theo from the evil Mouse King long enough to find out?

This short story retelling of "The Nutcracker and the Mouse King" is available for free when you sign up for my newsletter.

ACKNOWLEDGMENTS

On this page should be written very grand words describing the author's gratitude to her family, friends, and especially to her beta-readers, literature- and language-savvy friends who helped with the proposals, editor, cover designer, and others involved in the creation and beautification of her work. However, by grave mischance, a fairy's spell converted her glowing speech into a plain, ordinary "Thank you." Be assured, however, that those common words are no less heartfelt than the magnificent ones the author intended to grace this page.

ABOUT THE AUTHOR

E.J. KITCHENS loves tales of romance, adventure, and happily-ever-afters and strives to write such tales herself. When she's not thinking about dashing heroes or how awesome bacteria are—she is a microbiologist after all—she's enjoying the beautiful outdoors or talking about classic books and black-and-white movies. She is a member of Realm Makers and lives in Alabama.

May she beg a favor of you? You've already kindly read her book, would you also leave a review? Those gold stars can power more than fictional worlds: they encourage, inspire, and help authors through hurdles so we can seek out the people looking for books like ours. It's a daunting quest, and without you, fearless reader, it would fail. Will you join it? The map is before you:

http://www.amazon.com/review/create-review?&
asin=B07MKPQB4L

To learn more about E.J. Kitchens and her books, visit her website and sign up for her newsletter:
www.ElizabethJaneKitchens.com

Jane Austen Romance Meets Fairytale Adventure

When a prim, proper enchantress attempts to bewitch a magic mirror, she ends up cursed—powerless, penniless, dumped in a strange land, and stuck in the body of a hag. But the cure to her curse isn't what she expects, for one curse won't cure another. Or will it?

He's a non-magic who wants a respite from all things magical. She's an enchantress hiding a secret that could lead to her enslavement by the sorcerers. Together, they find themselves in a game of cat and mouse with the notorious Magic Thief.

Wanderer-turned-guard Athdar Owain has two secrets to keep and one to solve. Each could cost a life.

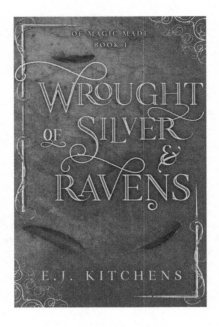

Athdar Owain is a hunted wanderer, one determined to keep his secrets and the treasure he carries safe at all costs. Princess Thea of Giliosthay is a Realm Walker. Betrayed by a trusted guard, her rare gift of enchantment is used to curse her brother and trap herself and her six sisters into a nightly dance with dragons in a secret Realm. Athdar alone can save them, but to trust enchanters is to risk exposure. And Athdar isn't sure where his loyalties lie.

Wrought of Silver and Ravens is a clean adventure-romance retelling of The Twelve Dancing Princesses set in The Magic Collectors story world.

Adventure and Romance Are Only a Page Away

E. J. Kitchens

Made in the USA
Coppell, TX
02 February 2022